My Regency Boyfriend

I0640369

LISA BOERO

ISBN: 978-0-9889900-7-4

Also by the author:

Murderers and Nerdy Girls Work Late

Bombers and Nerdy Girls Do Brunch

Kidnappers and Nerdy Girls Tie the Knot

"Kept afloat by a plucky heroine, like a yuppie version of Stephanie

Plum."

Kirkus Reviews

Hell Made Easy, the first book in the **Trilogy from Hell**

And the **Lady Althea Mystery Series** –

The Richmond Thief

The Ranleigh Question

For my fabulous book club, the Weekly Readers. Thanks for your support and encouragement.

Chapter 1

"**H**ey Sabby, how's it going?"

"What do you want Dave? You know I'm at work." Miss Sabrina March adjusted her thick tortoise shell glasses back up on her nose. Becky said they made her face look thinner, but at the moment they just felt heavy and annoying.

"What's a Led Zeppelin song for old people?"

"Stairlift to Heaven. And don't call me Sabby." Her family, and in particular her brother Dave, tended to call her Sab or Sabby even though they knew she didn't like it. Sab just sounded like sad or drab or mad. And Sabby – well *flabby* or *blabby* were really the best that could come out of that. And she still had those horrible memories of a childhood spent as the little fat girl taunted by more svelte children.

3

"*Sabby* just slipped out. Did I tell you that joke before?"

"No, but I'm smarter than you think. Speaking of, how much money do you need?" Dave never apologized unless he wanted something. And that something was usually always money, because lame heavy metal bands who toured the country playing dive bars and country fairs invariably needed cash. And because Dave knew she would do just about anything for her little brother.

"Just a hundred and I swear that this is the last time. The van broke down outside Independence and we need to get to St. Louis by tomorrow. If you wire it to me now, I can pay the mechanic to get started. The last gig didn't pay that much and the van has been guzzling gas like a mother."

Sabrina mumbled under her breath as she pulled up the Western Union website. " When are you going to pay me back for that hundred I sent you two months ago?"

"Right after this, I promise. We got a two-night gig this time. And the owner is friends with this guy who knows someone at Sony so this really could be our big break."

"Yeah, I know. You won't forget me at the top. I'm sending the money now, but seriously Dave you've tapped me out this time. I'm going to be eating Ramen noodles for the rest of the month at this rate."

Sabrina bit her lip and tasted the waxy coating of ChapStick she'd slathered on by way of makeup. It was Ramen noodles most nights anyway. Chicago was not cheap and her Junior Copywriter's salary, which had seemed astronomically large when compared with her previous employment at the university cafeteria, did not give her much wiggle room at the end of the month. Plus, the student loans had finally come home to roost. If she didn't need another reason to be depressed, the tab that showed up on her loan statements every month was enough to send her to therapy. That is what she got for not following her father into medicine as she had been expected to do. Unlike her other siblings, Sabrina had had the academic talents for pre-med. Unfortunately, her parents had refused to support her once she'd declared her major as English and dropped out of Biochemistry, saying that it didn't pay to throw money at a worthless degree.

Sabrina looked at the time on the screen – 12:20 – and felt her stomach growl. She cradled the phone on her shoulder and dug in her desk drawer until she unearthed the scrawny peanut butter sandwich she'd packed for today's delightful lunch. Really, it wasn't fair at all that her reduced circumstances hadn't made a dent in her rounded waistline. Poverty should at least have made her slim. Instead it had just added to the late-night pizza weight from college.

Sabrina heard a door open behind her cube. She turned just in time to see the newly hired VP of Marketing stride into his glass-walled office and shut the door. Her heart did a little flip and she sucked in her stomach as if that was going to do any good. Giles Philippe was literally the most attractive man Sabrina had ever been in the same room with – not technically the same room because she was in a cube and he had a corner office – but it didn't matter anyway. He'd never so much as looked in her direction since he'd come over three weeks ago from Belgium to plan the Federal Farm Machinery marketing reboot. The rumor around the office was that he had been hand-selected by the new CEO, Red Carson.

Giles was the kind of man who looked like he'd stepped out of a romance novel, with his high cheekbones and firm chin. His hair was dark and wavy; longer than a stuffy corporation like Federal Farm Machinery would

7

normally tolerate. It gave him an edge that Sabrina found

incredibly exciting. And he had that hint of self-assured

twinkle in his deep brown eyes that made Sabrina think that

underneath the perfect face lurked an intelligent brain. He

was also tall and lean, with just enough definition in his

broad shoulders to show he worked out. She wondered

when he found the time. Then again, he didn't have a

wedding ring so maybe he was single. It was her experience

that single guys could always make time for themselves. In

any case, none of the single guys she'd come across in the

last couple of years had had more than a passing interest in

her.

　　With his height, Giles might even look good in

breeches and a form-fitting frock coat like all of the heroes

in the Austen-type books that littered the floor of Sabrina's

sad little bedroom. Sabrina had been a fan since she'd been

old enough to read between the lines of the sometimes

chaste stories. It didn't take much to imagine all sorts of

things beyond the final kiss. Then again, her favorite book of all time, *To Kiss an Earl*, by Paige Lindsey, was one of those that spelled a few things out beyond the joyful marriage of Miss Sabrina Dunhill and the Earl of March. Ms. Lindsey had seen fit to describe in detail a slow lingering kiss and some very hot dialog as they found each other's arms in the marriage bed. And it was just too fantastic that a book would have just the right combination of names – Sabrina, Lady March. Imagine – that could be her!

Plus, the Earl of March was a hero Sabrina could enthusiastically endorse. Ms. Lindsey described him as blond, handsome, rich and intelligent. In addition, he was interested in new technology for the improvement of harvests on his estates and fully conscious of the disadvantageous position women had in Georgian society. Sabrina had read the book a couple of hundred times.

Whenever she felt sad or lonely, she would open the dog-eared pages and lose herself in a feisty heroine and the intelligent soulful man who finally wins her heart. It was even now on her nightstand, opened to page 103, where March sees Sabrina Dunhill at Almack's. He is instantly drawn to her luscious dark hair and sumptuous figure, and dances with her despite the claims of several more worthy damsels and Miss Dunhill's own dangerous reputation.

Unfortunately, Sabrina was not Lady March, but just another one of the lowly peons set to work on transforming Federal Farm Machinery from a stodgy backwater of farm equipment into a modern-day agricultural marvel. Agricultural marvel – Sabrina liked the sound of that phrase. Maybe she'd use it in one of the many webpages she'd been tasked to fill with content. She snuck a peek at Giles' office. He was on the phone again – probably some important conference with the CEO. He was writing furious notes on a legal pad.

Sabrina turned back and reconnected with Dave's long explanation of the set they'd played the night before.

"So then Kevin said we should do 'Angels in the Dust' but I said no way because you can't do two power ballads in a row. People get bored with that stuff," Dave said.

Sabrina heard the sound of Giles' door open behind her and hastily minimized Western Union and got off the phone. One had to look busy in front of management. She looked steadily at her computer, trying desperately not to seem as nervous as she always felt whenever she even caught a glimpse of Giles. She could feel his eyes on her back, which was natural since she was the only one still at her desk in the immediate vicinity. That was a plus that Sabrina hadn't previously considered – she looked like a hard worker just because she couldn't afford to eat out for the lunch break.

"Um, Miss." Giles' soft accent made even the most commonplace words sound like an invitation to sin.

Sabrina took a deep breath to steady her nerves and then turned around. "Yes?" It was clear that Giles couldn't recall her name. "March. Sabrina March."

"Yes, Miss March. Here." He thrust the notepad in her direction. "I want you to find the survey data on the last two campaigns. And I need a rundown of costs, sales, consumer engagement – whatever files there are."

Sabrina hesitated a moment, pretty sure Giles didn't realize that Junior Copywriters didn't prepare reports like the one he was envisioning. This was supposed to be the work of the staff of Marilyn Townsend, the Director of Consumer Engagement; a sixty-something woman who had parlayed her childhood on a farm into an entire career of looking busy. Then again, Giles was the boss of Sabrina's boss' boss.

"Okay. Sure," Sabrina replied. Becky would know where to get the data. Becky was in finance on the second floor and had worked at Federal long enough to know where the bodies were buried.

Giles seemed relieved at her easy compliance. "Good. Tomorrow morning will be fine. I have a meeting at nine o'clock, so come to my office before then." He turned on his heel and marched back into his office while Sabrina attempted to control a major panic attack.

Giles sat back at his desk and pulled out his phone. Nothing. Not a text message or missed call or anything. Then again, he didn't know why he expected something different. Helene had said it was over, and she'd clearly meant it. Besides, wasn't this job in Chicago supposed to be a fresh start? If things hadn't gone so wrong with Helene, Giles wouldn't have even considered the move – not when he could have gone anywhere. After his work with the

Legends campaign, he had his pick of offers. They said no one but Giles could have taken a sleepy suitcase business with a couple of ideas for purses and turned it into the producer of the *It* handbag – the one no starlet in Hollywood would be caught dead without. That wasn't anything but the most skillful marketing campaign the business had seen in a long time. Louis Vuitton wanted him so badly that they'd made him an offer even he didn't believe. And yet, instead of taking them up on it, he had opted for the Federal Farm Machinery offer because Chicago and farm machinery was as far away as he could get from the woman who had crushed his heart beneath the heel of her stiletto.

Giles threw the phone onto the desk and caught sight of that girl he'd just given an assignment to through the clear part of the frosted glass walls of his office. Sabrina March. She was gesturing with her hand while she talked to someone on the phone. Then she flung the phone down

14

and lunged out of her cube, nearly tripping over her chair.

He smiled as her short form bobbed and weaved through

the cubes, heading, he guessed, to the elevator. She was

what he'd imagined all American girls would be like when

he'd gone to Harvard for college. Sweet and polite.

Rounded in a way the flat-chested twig-thin European girls

could never hope to be. Natural in their fresh cheeks and

broad smiles. Although, Sabrina hadn't actually smiled at

him. She looked at him as if he might take a bite out of her

pale skin. Probably because he'd given her an assignment

completely out of her narrow job description and way

above her pay grade. That's what you got for skipping lunch

and working harder than your own boss – more

opportunity for growth.

Chapter 2

I t was one in the morning when Sabrina finally crawled up the three flights of stairs to her apartment. She'd spent hours with Becky, who, bless her heart, had dropped everything to help Sabrina pull information on practically every aspect of all the advertising for the last five years. It was grueling, it was exhausting, it was endless, and it really showed just how little imagination the marketing folks had at Federal Farm Machinery. Seriously, if Sabrina saw one more cowboy-hatted leather-skinned twenty-something on a tractor, she thought she would scream.

Were hunks on machines all they could come up with? Probably that's why they'd hired Giles the wunderkind. Everyone knew about the Legends campaign and if you didn't, all you had to do was buy a fashion magazine and the ads would be all over it. But it wasn't just ads, it was digital, social media, you name it. But why he'd moved over to farm machinery was anyone's guess.

Sabrina felt so tired that she almost stumbled over the package set inside her door. The manager of the building, Mr. Nelson, was a grandfatherly man who'd looked out for Sabrina ever since the day she moved in. It was just like him to make sure she got her mail even when she hadn't gotten around to checking the box downstairs. Sabrina picked it up and blinked at the return address. Her mother. What did her mother want now?

Sabrina's mother was the kind of woman who would have done well in the 1950's. Her hair was always perfect. The house was always perfect. She wore heels to do even the most mundane activities, including all of the charitable committees from which she dominated the social life of Manville, Illinois. As the wife of the most respected doctor in town, she felt it to be her duty.

And she expected children who would tow the same hard rigidly proper line. Unfortunately, neither Sabrina nor Dave had lived up to any of the expectations their older sister, Tiffany, assumed with ease. It was why they'd stuck together and why Sabrina still took Dave's phone calls even after his sense of fun had moved him to torture her with bad jokes, puns and pranks of all kinds. He was still her lovable younger brother, and Sabrina could never stay mad for long.

Tiffany was as beautiful and put-together as a model in a catalog – blond and tall, with straight white teeth and ram-rod posture. She'd gotten a business degree and now sold houses. Her sunny blonde Barbie face was even on a billboard in Manville. Sabrina's mother had never been so proud.

Sabrina harkened back a generation and was, unfortunately for her, a spitting image of her plump, short, dark-haired grandmother on her father's side, Pearl Freiberg. Sabrina dearly loved Grandma Pearl – her death six months ago still made Sabrina cry when she thought of it – but no one would have ever called Pearl a beauty. Smart, yes. Pearl had studied law back when women didn't do those sorts of things and, despite marriage and children, forged her own small estate planning practice. It was said that Pearl had a knack for knowing just what her clients would need. Her perspicacity kept the family afloat, and Sabrina's father in medical school, when Grandfather March got sick and died from his two-pack-a-day habit.

Sabrina grabbed the package and dragged herself into her room. She sagged down on the bed and ripped at the cardboard box. Inside she found another small jewelry box. She pulled open the lid and a gold pendant glittered up at her. Sabrina whistled through her teeth. The pendant was a circle with a cross in the middle and looked handmade and old. The box also included a note from her mother that read:

Finally went through the safe deposit box. Not sure when Grandma Pearl got this, but she wore it all the time. She told your father that she wanted you to have it. Not sure why, but here you go.

Mom

Sabrina held the pendant in her hand for a moment. A memory, so vivid it was if time had stood still, flashed in front of her eyes. She was six years old, sitting on her grandmother's lap, listening to her tell some story about grandmother's grandmother and the beautiful house they had once owned, with a garden and birds. It was a magical place, full of possibilities. Even all of these years later,

Sabrina could remember the sweet spicy scent of her grandmother's perfume and feel the warmth of her skin. Sabrina caught sight of the necklace and touched it with her pudgy child finger.

"Someday, this will be yours," Grandmother Pearl had said to her. "Choose your dreams carefully."

Sabrina slipped the fine gold chain around her neck and fastened the clasp, feeling good to have something from her grandmother close to her heart. Choose your dreams carefully. Well, right now her dream was to sleep. She readied for bed and then got in under the covers.

She caught sight of *To Kiss an Earl* and picked it up, flipping to the racy part at the end. The Earl of March with his strong arms and soft lips – Sabrina Dunhill, locked in a heavenly embrace, about to experience the most magical night of her life. Sabrina drifted off to sleep, dreaming of the Earl of March. If only he were a real live person, ready to fulfill Sabrina's every desire.

March kissed her slowly, reverently, probing the contours of her full lips. Sabrina resisted at first, unsure of the strange sensations the earl's kiss awakened in her. The warmth spread throughout her body and pooled down deep inside her. She moved even farther into his arms. Her heart sped up in anticipation. She parted her lips, succumbing to the insistent pressure of his mouth, and March deepened the kiss. They were joined together at last, bound by a desire so strong, Sabrina felt as if she might melt into him. It was the most wonderful, delicious dream. She never wanted to wake up.

Dream? Sabrina sat up with a start.

"What is the matter, my darling?" the man she had just been kissing said. In the faint light filtered through the bedroom curtains, Sabrina could just make out his handsome angular face.

Sabrina screamed and fell out of bed, landing with a thump on the cold floor. She scrambled to her feet and rubbed her eyes, hoping she was still asleep. "Who are you and what are you doing in my bed?"

The man eyed her, an amused smile playing about his perfect lips. "Come my love, surely you can't forget me so easily. I am your husband after all."

"Husband?" Sabrina took a step back towards the door. "But I'm not married."

"So you forget even our wedding, do you?" He smiled at her archly. "Perhaps then I should introduce myself." He inclined his head in a mock bow. "The Earl of March at your service, Miss Dunhill."

"Miss Dunhill? No, seriously, who are you? Did Dave set this up? Are you a friend of his?" Dave had a weird sense of humor, so anything was possible. Although this went way beyond any previous practical joke.

23

"Who is this Dave of which you speak?"

"This is so not funny!" Sabrina took another step back and nearly fell backwards as a paperback romance slid out from under her foot.

The man leaped out of bed as if to catch her but stopped as soon as she shrieked, "Not one step closer or I swear I will hurt you!"

The man cocked his head to one side and crossed his arms over his chest. He was dressed in a long cotton shirt of some kind. However, given what she could see from the way it hugged his body in all the right places, he was wearing nothing else. His eyes held hers with an expression of love and tenderness so intense that Sabrina had to look away. This guy was a phenomenal actor.

"Hurt me?" he said. "But my dear, haven't we hurt each other enough? I will never forget your face when you told me that I could never win your heart. Do not tell me that you now regret your choice? Such feelings I have for

24

you can never be extinguished. I throw my heart, my soul and everything I possess at your feet, my dearest Sabrina."

"Ugh!" Sabrina made a dash for the door and then slammed it behind her. She had to get away from this crazy man, whoever he thought he was. But where could she go? Then she caught sight of the clock. 7:15? Oh my God! Forget the nut in her bedroom, she had to get to work. Now!

She ran back into the room, almost colliding with the Earl of Whoever he thought he was. She shoved past him and started pulling clothes out of her closet.

"Look, I don't know who you are or what you think you are doing here, but I have to go." She hastily threw a dress over her head and stubbed her feet into a pair of black flats. "When I get back, you better be gone. I mean it! If you aren't I will call the police!"

"Police? Who is that?" he said.

She ignored him and ran out of the room, grabbing her purse and her keys. Dave was so dead. She really didn't have time for any of this nonsense. "Lock the door behind you," she called out as she dashed down the stairs.

Once she was on the El, she tried to pull herself together. If she could just get through her meeting with Giles, and then get through the rest of the day, she could deal with the man in her apartment. Probably he would be gone by the time she got home. No friend of Dave's would want to hang around once the joke was done. Unless he really was an out of work actor – in which case there wasn't anything she had that was worth stealing – and he was welcome to all the peanut butter, bread and Ramen noodles he could eat. She called Dave's number, but he didn't pick up, so she left him a message, telling him to call her.

Giles watched Sabrina through the clear edge of the frosted glass wall as she gathered up a stack of papers and pushed her thick dark hair out of her eyes with an anxious hand. He couldn't see her face but felt sure it wore a worried frown. He'd been like that when he'd taken his first job – nervous and anxious to please. But one good idea followed the next and his promotions flowed so fast that he didn't have time to worry about whether he really had the credentials to do what they asked him to do. Success began to seem like a foregone conclusion.

She knocked timidly at his door and shuffled in; her arms piled high with papers. He indicated that she should sit and she did warily, perched on the edge of her chair.

"So, what is all this?" He gestured to the papers.

She swallowed hard and then looked down, obviously trying to regain her composure. Her glasses were too big for her face and slid down her nose. She pushed them back with a finger. "It's what you asked for. I have the finance part." She pulled some papers out of the stack.

27

"See, here is what we spent on the two campaigns." She pushed the papers across the desk without managing to make eye contact.

Giles picked them up, pretending to study them, but really just waiting for her to go on.

"And these are the sales figures." She pushed another set of papers over to him. "I can put them together in a spreadsheet if you like, but I'm afraid I didn't have time yesterday." At that she looked up timidly. "I'm sorry."

He waved his hand. "Not necessary just yet. Go on."

Her voice became more confident. "Here is a summary of the consumer engagement. They did surveys before during and after both campaigns."

"Continue."

"The rest of this is documentation related to the ads themselves – the magazines and newspapers and industry trade shows."

28

"Okay." He looked at her intently, forcing her to meet his gaze. "So, help me Miss March, what does all this data tell you?"

She stared back at him with a blank wide-eyed look. Her blue eyes were magnified by the glasses. She had lovely eyes he realized, deep blue like the color of the ocean on a rainy day. "Miss March?"

She swallowed. "Yes, um, sorry, what was the question?"

"What is your conclusion after reviewing the data you've given me?"

"Oh. Yes. They didn't work very well. The campaigns I mean. Our sales have continued to drop."

"And why do you think that is?" This is what he'd asked every manager and sub-manager since he'd arrived at Federal, and no one, but no one, could give him a straight answer. He'd decided to go to the bottom to see if he could uncover some honesty. And Miss Sabrina Marsh, with her obvious dedication to the job, had seemed just the person to tell him what she thought. Besides, he had a hunch that she just might be able to confirm his own theories if he could get her to open up a little.

She took a deep breath and then said in a rush, "I'm technically not trained in marketing, but I have to say that our last two campaigns, and the ones prior to that because I checked back for the last decade, seem to be selling the same thing."

He smiled at her and said in an encouraging voice. "And what is that?"

She blushed suddenly – the pink sweeping up to the roots of her hair. Now this was interesting. He leaned in, curious as to what could make her color up like that.

She looked down shyly. "Sex. Virility. You've got nothing but hot young guys in plaid shirts and cowboy hats, riding big shiny machines. If that isn't a metaphor then I'm not an English Major, which I was, so there it is." She picked up speed, getting into the argument. "And I don't think most farmers, not real farmers, care about how sexy their tractor is. I mean, they are trying to make a living and these machines cost a huge amount of money. They are an investment, not something you buy just because your days of life without Viagra are over." And then as if realizing she'd been too frank, put her hand over her mouth.

Giles started to laugh. And laugh and laugh.

Sabrina said "I'm sorry. I let my tongue get away from me. That wasn't what I should have said."

He wiped his eyes. "No, Miss March, do not apologize for anything you have said. I agree completely."

"You do?" She let out her breath and sat back in the chair, limp as a rag doll.

Her look of relief was so ridiculously genuine that he might have laughed again. Instead, he smiled at her and

31

watched as a reciprocal smile lit up her face. "When I looked at the data, I came to the same conclusion. We are selling sex instead of tractors. Unfortunately, given my work with Legends, I think that they hired me expecting more of the same. But handbags are not tractors, are they?"

"No."

"So, what are we going to do about it?" he said.

"Figure out what drives our customers' decisions and then market to that?"

"Exactly. From now on Miss March, you will be on special assignment to me."

"But Marilyn will —"

"I'll deal with Marilyn and your supervisor. Besides, I won't need all your time – it will be ad hoc. Try to fit my requests in with your regular work. Do you understand?"

Sabrina nodded. "I can do that."

Giles looked at his watch. "Almost nine o'clock. Here take all your work and file it away somewhere just in case we need to look back. Or better yet, get one of the assistants to scan it for you."

Sabrina gathered the paperwork in her arms and stood. Giles came around the desk and opened the door. "A pleasure working with you, Miss March."

"Sabrina is fine."

"Sabrina, call me Giles."

She nodded and then passed through the door. Giles followed her out and headed towards the boardroom.

Sabrina could feel the icy stares on her as she walked back to her desk and set the mass of documents beside her computer. Mindy, a Senior Copywriter in the cube next to Sabrina, stuck her head around the cube wall. "What was that all about?"

Half a dozen heads popped up over the cube walls like a pack of prairie dogs coming up out of their burrows.

"Mr. Philippe handed me this marketing project yesterday while you guys were at lunch. I guess I was the only one available at the time. Who knows?"

"Doesn't he know you're in Copywriting?" Mindy said.

"I guess so. I wasn't going to tell him I couldn't do it."

They all nodded knowingly and then popped back down when Marilyn's voice could be cut through the hum of other conversations. Marilyn would chew out the Copywriting Supervisor if employees didn't seem busy enough.

Chapter 3

When Sabrina finally opened the door of her apartment at 7:30, it was dark. Good. Whoever he was had obviously gone. She checked her phone. Dave still hadn't called back. She flipped on the light and then promptly dropped her purse. "What are you still doing here?"

The man, dressed as before in a long nightshirt, sat huddled in a chair by the window. He turned to her, his brow furrowed and his eyes blinking at the light. "What is this place you have brought me to Sabrina? Where is March Hall or the house in Grosvenor Square?"

"Oh come off it. I'm too tired for this joke," Sabrina replied

"What joke? Where are we?" His eyes bore into hers, pleading. He seemed genuinely lost and afraid. Seriously, the guy could get an Oscar for his performance.

Sabrina took a step closer, deciding to play along until he would give up the act. "The right question is, when are we? And the answer is 200 years from the date of your marriage. We are in Chicago, Illinois, which sits right in the middle of the United States of America."

"The colonies?" He stood up quickly.

"Yes. Now a large country that spans the continent."

"But England?"

"Is still around. You're just not there."

"And how are we here, dearest Sabrina?"

Sabrina threw up her hands in frustration. "I don't know why or how you're here. But I'm here because I grew up in Manville and went to college at Northwestern and

36

then rented this apartment when I got a job at Federal Farm Machinery. And I'm not your Sabrina!"

He sat back down as if her words had knocked the wind out of him and covered his face with his hands. "This must be a dream, or I am going mad. For the last thing I remember, I had come to your chamber because it was our wedding night. And I had never felt so happy in all my years as when I saw you in my bed waiting for me, with your beautiful clear eyes and midnight hair." He looked up. "But now you say that you are not mine and how can that be when you have the same midnight hair and fine eyes and your skin is like silk."

He gazed at her with such a look of desire that, even though Sabrina knew it was completely crazy, she felt her bones start to melt.

"The curves of your figure are like to drive any man wild."

Sabrina glanced down reflexively at her heavy breasts and rounded stomach. "Really?"

The man continued on. "So you must be my wife, dearest Sabrina, because if you are not I shall die."

That was something Sabrina never thought she'd hear from the lips of a man. She could feel her resistance weakening. At least he seemed harmless, and she wasn't in the mood to try to explain the whole situation to the police. When Dave called her back, she'd straighten it out.

"Well, if you are going to stay, we should eat something. Why were you sitting in the dark?"

"I had no notion how to light these lamps and no flint to do it. Do you not have candles in this house?" he said.

"The lights aren't candles. They are electricity."

"Electricity!" His eyes lit up. "As in the force that activates lightening?"

"Yes."

"I have read of experiments to test the power of lightening but never thought to see it so ingeniously used!" He stood to examine the overhead fixture and Sabrina realized that he wasn't as tall as she imagined; 5' 10" at the most. This was still taller than Sabrina's shrimpy 5'2", but certainly not Giles' powerful frame. Then again, weren't people in the past much shorter? But he wasn't from the past. He couldn't be. Perhaps this was all a dream – a fantasy in her head that had run amok. Hadn't she always felt like she knew the characters of *To Kiss an Earl* intimately?

"And how does one light it?" he said.

Sabrina walked over to the wall and flipped the switch on and off.

"Amazing! If I had not seen it with my own eyes. I would never have believed it. My dear, this world is wondrous indeed."

"I am wondrous hungry, so let me see what I can make for dinner," Sabrina replied.

"Make?" He looked horrified. "But those fine hands should not cook. Are there no servants in this world to take care of such matters?"

"Not in my pay grade, but it's a lot less work than it used to be." She walked over to the kitchenette part of her small one bedroom and pulled open the refrigerator.

The man followed close on her heels and peered anxiously over her shoulder. "What is this box?"

"Refrigerator. It keeps food cold so that it doesn't spoil."

"With ice?"

"With electricity, but don't ask me how it works because I couldn't tell you. Want some spaghetti with red sauce?"

He gave her a blank look.

"You'll like it, I promise." Sabrina took out a jar of spaghetti sauce that was three fourths full and set it on the counter. Then she reached up and got down a box of spaghetti.

The man followed her progress with wide-eyed wonder. He asked about the microwave and the electric burners and disposal. Sabrina tried to explain the mechanism of each as best she could but couldn't shake the feeling that he was sincere in his professions of ignorance. Did he have amnesia? No, that couldn't be it because he knew things about England that were correct or would have been correct two hundred years ago – like the fact that one shouldn't drink the water. It had taken her fifteen minutes of cajoling before he would accept a glass of tap water from her.

Finally, they sat down to dinner at the rickety card table Sabrina had tried to spruce up with a hand-me-down tablecloth. The man tucked into his spaghetti with relish.

"This food is beyond anything I have ever eaten. I had something similar once when I was on the Grand Tour, but nothing in Italy was as wonderful as this. I apprehend that the sauce is made from the tomato, or love apple as they sometimes call it, which is very fitting do you not think?"

"It is nothing really," she replied uncomfortably.

He reached his hand out and took Sabrina's fingers in his. "You are too modest my love. The noodles are so thin and the sauce so sweet and ripe, that one does not need many courses to round out the meal."

"Courses?"

But he continued on, "Although some pheasant would accompany this quite nicely."

42

Sabrina pulled her hand away. "There is no pheasant here, sorry."

"No? We must see about shooting some."

"No, we must not. Chicago is a city not the country," she replied.

"I thought I saw some fly past the window this afternoon. They were small, I grant you, but certainly worth eating."

Sabrina put down her fork. "Those were pigeons, and you are not allowed to shoot them in the city."

"A pity, that."

Sabrina didn't reply but instead picked up his plate and gave him a third helping of spaghetti. When he was safely chewing and couldn't reply, she said, "I suppose I should let you stay here until we get this mess sorted out, but if I do, you will have to get some decent clothes. Do you have anything but that nightshirt with you?" And then a thought struck her. "Please tell me you know how to use the bathroom."

He smiled. "If you mean the water closet, then yes. I am not sure how you have managed to pump the water from the cistern into the room, but I did play with the levers enough to assess their function. It is truly an amazing invention."

"Thank goodness. But as I was saying, do you have any other clothes?"

He gave her an intense look. "One does not wear outer clothes on one's wedding night."

Sabrina felt her face flush and swallowed hard. He had charisma, whoever he was. "And what should I call you? I mean, I can't call you the Earl of March all the time."

"My given name is Oliver, as I think I have mentioned before, but you may call me March if Oliver is too familiar for a husband."

Sabrina didn't know what that was supposed to mean, as one really should be very familiar with one's husband, but replied. "Oliver will do just fine."

They lapsed into uncomfortable silence. Finally, Oliver said, "I sense a certain hesitation, my love." He studied her face. "It occurs to me that you may be suffering from the natural timidity a gently-bred woman feels upon her wedding night."

Sabrina took a sip of water trying to figure out how she should respond. It occurred to her that virginity might be just the excuse she needed. And really, her experience had been so limited, and so frankly disappointing, that she might as well have been a virgin. "I am afraid that you have discovered my secret, Oliver. As much as I may want to consummate the marriage, my natural modesty holds me back. Do have patience with me, I beg of you."

Oliver nodded solemnly. "I promise I shall not press you further until such time as you can give yourself to me." He smiled at her. "But I shall do all that is in my power to make sure that time is soon upon us."

After dinner, Sabrina showed Oliver how to dry the dishes and put them away in the cupboard. Then they dug around in Sabrina's room, looking for a tee shirt, some jeans and flip flops Dave had left by mistake when he'd crashed for a week with Sabrina in between gigs.

Oliver held the tee shirt up critically. "I have to assume that this is an undergarment of some sort. And what are these pictures? Are they magical creatures?" He pointed to Gene Simmons in full Kiss regalia.

"No, it is a shirt. But the men are simply dressed in costumes. They are musicians, but with a theatrical sort of thing."

Oliver nodded. "I saw Keene's performance of Hamlet once. Amazing how they made him up."

46

Sabrina smiled. "I'm sure that was just like Kiss. Here." She handed him the jeans. "Go try these on. They just might fit." She looked at Oliver – the nightshirt clinging suggestively to his every muscle. "Oh wait, you'll need underwear." She racked her brain. Did she have something from the few losers she'd slept with? Or had Dave left her anything? It was a negative on both counts and Sabrina certainly wasn't going to hand Oliver a pair of hers. "Never mind," she said. "Commando it is."

Oliver looked at her strangely, but she shooed him into the bathroom. When he emerged, Sabrina didn't know whether to laugh or to pant. It was clear that Dave had never had enough sinewy muscle to fill out the shirt and the jeans. Well, one couldn't blame a girl for staring. They were so tight they looked like they'd been painted on.

Oliver caught her look. "These pantaloons are rather snug. Are they meant to be so? For I am afraid I am

47

unaccustomed to such an exhibition. And how are they to be fastened? There is only one button."

"Here. This is a zipper and it closes by pulling up on the metal tab."

Oliver tried unsuccessfully several times, and Sabrina reluctantly zipped up the fly for him while trying not to notice the encouraging size of his assets. The jeans were even tighter than before.

She sighed. "Tomorrow you and I can go shopping. For now, you probably want to take a shower and get back into that nightshirt. I can't imagine those jeans are comfortable enough to sleep in."

"A shower of rain? How is that to be achieved?"

"Not rain, but something like. Come with me and I'll show you how it works."

He was duly impressed with the mechanism and the even temperature of the water and so Sabrina gave him a towel and left him to his ablutions.

She left another message for Dave and then set her mind to the problem of the sleeping arrangements.

Chapter 4

Giles flipped on the light of his expensive apartment. The apartment felt cold and uninviting, but he hadn't had the time to even buy furniture. He'd kept his apartment in Brussels and didn't ship anything over, preferring to have a clean slate to work with. The result was bare rooms and a sad sinking feeling whenever he walked in the door. Maybe tomorrow he'd finally go out and select something. Or maybe not. He hardly left the office anyway. What did it matter what his apartment looked like?

He pulled his cell phone out of his jacket pocket and dialed the Thai place that delivered, ordering a curry with extra rice. That task complete, Giles wandered into his bedroom and shrugged out of his coat and tie. The bed was rumpled from where he had had a fitful sleep the night

before. He had a momentary flash of memory – Helene
tangled in the sheets after that first night they spent
together, the rounded form of her breasts apparent under
the dark fabric and the surge of animal desire he'd felt just
watching her sleep. He cursed himself, realizing that he felt
hard even thinking about her. He needed to move on.

Unfortunately, the job at Federal Farm Machinery
didn't leave much time for the casual hookups that had
been his mainstay throughout his twenties. And in any case,
he didn't have the energy to pull off the Casanova act.
Maybe this is what the thirties did to you. It forced you into
monogamy because the other option was just too damn
tiring. Except that he couldn't even count on a steady
girlfriend to buoy him up. Helene was the only one he
wanted.

Truth be told, he was struggling at work as well.
The meeting with the Chairman of the Board had not gone

well. Apparently, the CEO had hired Giles without the Board's full support. Today, the conflict came out in the open. The Chairman informed Giles that he had six months to turn the marketing around or he would find himself out of a job. Six months! That wasn't enough time to undo twenty years of lack-luster performance.

A rational man would simply call up Louis Vuitton and get out of Chicago before it was too late, but Giles had never been rational. He lived by gut instinct and his gut instinct told him that turning Federal around would seal his reputation for the rest of his career. He had to figure out how to tap into the demand that he knew was out there.

The buzzer sounded and Giles gave instructions for the food to be sent up. He sat at the kitchen island because he didn't have a table and ate his food while he read emails on his phone. Then he pulled out his laptop to review the data he'd gathered on the prior campaigns. He felt a twinge of guilt that he'd made Sabrina March pull all of the data herself, but it was probably good for her to learn more about the business. In any case, she'd come to the same conclusions he had. He smiled as he thought about her little speech. How she'd blushed. It had been a long time since he'd seen a woman blush. The women he dated weren't the innocent type.

Giles wondered idly what Sabrina was doing at that moment – probably alone in her apartment like him. She had that look of a long-term single girl. It was a certain slump of the shoulders and an air of resignation that hung around her like an aura, as if a shoebox apartment and several cats was the best she could possibly hope for. Then again, who was he to talk? Giles turned back to the computer. At least there was always work to keep him occupied.

At that moment, Sabrina was wishing she lived alone with cats, because she was finding it a bit difficult to convince Oliver to sleep on the couch. She was also finding it hard to meet his eyes because the towel around his hips kept slipping.

"My love, surely there is no need to exclude me so cruelly from your chamber. For you know I have pledged my word not to claim my privileges until you are ready."

"I know you have promised, but I really would feel more comfortable if you slept out here," Sabrina replied.

Oliver put his hands firmly on her shoulders. His eyes held hers in a smoldering gaze. "Sabrina. You are my wife and I love you more than words can properly address, but in this you shall not deny me."

Sabrina blinked. No man had ever looked at her like that, which probably meant that sleeping next to him was a really bad idea. Then again, he'd promised to behave so perhaps there wasn't any harm in sleeping wrapped in the warmth of a man's arms – particularly one as handsome as Oliver. The whole wife thing was a problem, however. "I don't know if it is such a good idea."

Oliver pulled her close and she found her head resting against his chest. She could hear the beating of his heart. Her own seemed to skip a beat. "My darling, I am a man of my word. Nothing will happen between us."

Oh, what the Hell! Sabrina felt the towel pressed up against her slide dangerously down his hips. She smiled. "Fine, but let's get that nightshirt back on you."

Sabrina banished Oliver to the bathroom and closed her bedroom door. She dug in her drawer, looking for that high-necked flannel nightgown she often wore to bed in the middle of winter. She found it and then located a jogging bra she wouldn't feel too uncomfortable sleeping in. She noticed that she was still wearing her grandmother's pendant and took that off so that she wouldn't break the delicate gold chain. She prepared for bed and caught sight of herself in the mirror. Hideous. Absolutely hideous. The nightgown hung straight from her shoulders, both drowning her small frame and making it look twice as wide. The jogging bra compressed all of her flesh into one massive shelf that jiggled in slow undulations like a waterbed when she walked. One look at her was probably the best contraceptive she could have come up with. She waited outside the bathroom door for Oliver, confident that they would both get a good night's sleep.

Oliver opened the door and gave her a slow once over. Sabrina waited for the snide comment, but instead he said with a voice so sincere that it couldn't be a joke, "You are the most beautiful woman I have ever known and yet at every moment you become more beautiful still."

Sabrina blushed furiously. "Ah, thanks." She dashed by him into the bathroom, where several rounds of cold water finally doused her flaming cheeks. This was going to be a long night.

Despite her fears, Sabrina woke refreshed. As she slowly untangled herself from Oliver's arms, she realized that she probably hadn't slept that well in years. Maybe having him around for a little while longer wouldn't be so bad. That is if they could get him some decent clothes.

After a breakfast that was punctuated by a long discussion as to why the people of the future ate tiny pieces of bread with milk instead of a proper breakfast like steak and beer, they set out from her apartment. Unfortunately, they didn't get very far because Oliver stood transfixed on the sidewalk, his eyes almost out of their sockets with wonder. "What are these miraculous things?"

"What?"

Oliver pointed to the traffic.

"Cars," Sabrina replied. "I mean, horseless carriages. They have engines in them that are powered by burning petroleum."

"Petroleum?"

"Yes, but don't ask me to explain how it works." Sabrina took Oliver's arm and pulled him forward. "Now follow me and you won't get hit by one of them"

Oliver could not contain his excitement at every new technology he encountered. The El was amazing. The streetlights were a wonder. Cars and motorcycles defied description. Even the road pavement met with his approval. It was so smooth and produced no dust or mud as the cars drove over it. His enthusiasm felt contagious, and made Sabrina realize just how much she took for granted in her life.

They arrived at the store – one of those discounted seconds-type places – and took the elevator up to the Men's section. Sabrina had always hated these stores with their white linoleum and fluorescent lighting. They made her feel bad even before she tried on the clothes that would inevitably not fit her properly. Her petite frame and her abundant curves put her squarely in the black hole of clothing. Everything was both too long and too tight, and so she opted for shift dresses that hung down on her past the knee and cardigan sweaters with sleeves pushed up her arm like an extra from Miami Vice, pared with some uninspiring but comfortable black flats.

She was in one of those dresses today and, as she caught sight of herself in the mirrored elevator walls, she cringed. Oliver, on the other hand, looked like a model. It was amazing, even bad clothes couldn't damage such a lovely specimen. Sabrina felt a flicker of excitement wick up her spine. Shopping for Oliver was probably going to be a lot of fun because he would make everything look good.

Oliver couldn't believe the amount of clothing or the fact one could just purchase items readymade. "Why, my tailor would take weeks to make a jacket!" he exclaimed when he saw a rack of suit coats.

Sabrina guided him back into casual wear. It was more appropriate for her budget. Then came the problem of sizes. Sabrina eyed him suspiciously. He might be a large or a medium depending on the garment. She held up a pair of athletic shorts. "Do you think these would fit you?"

Oliver took one look at them and started to laugh and laugh and laugh. He doubled over, slapping his thighs.

Sabrina stood there woodenly. "What is so funny?"

Oliver wiped his eyes with his hand. "I shall not malign the manhood of these future men, but I was breeched low these many years. How can you ask me to become a child again?"

"Fine. Let's look for jeans." And when he gave her a quizzical look, she added, "Pants made of jean. Like what you are wearing – only perhaps not quite so tight."

She found several pairs of jeans and a couple of tee shirts that didn't have Gene Simmons' tongue all over them and marched Oliver into the dressing room.

Oliver emerged, looking like a runway model in a pair of hipster skinny jeans that only a man with a fine pair of legs could pull off. The tee shirt fit him with just the right amount of careless ease. Sabrina whipped out her phone and snapped a picture while he wasn't looking. Seriously, Oliver was amazingly handsome in normal clothes. Of course, Sabrina longed to dress him in really fine men's clothes – a suit or a tux with the tie undone, like she'd just gotten him home from a party and couldn't resist unwrapping the package – but she didn't have that kind of money to waste on a stranger.

Sabrina urged Oliver to try on more and was not disappointed with the results. Black jeans with a tough guy edge topped with a plain white tee shirt that fitted his chest to perfection. James Dean eat your heart out. Faded boot legged jeans with a blue tee shirt just the color of his eyes. And even straight jeans looked good on him – the way they hung off his hips suggestively. Sabrina surreptitiously snapped one photo after another, finding herself enjoying shopping for the first time ever.

That is until she heard a familiar voice. "Sabrina! What are you doing here?"

"Oh hey, Mindy. Nice to see you," Sabrina lied.

Mindy pointedly looked at the men's clothes. "Shopping for someone?"

Sabrina opened her mouth to reply, but at that moment Oliver walked out of the dressing rooms with an even more attractive pair of dark-washed slim-fit jeans and the blue tee shirt.

"I find these most pleasing," he said to Sabrina. "They are not stiff like the other ones."

Mindy's mouth dropped open and Sabrina felt a swell of borrowed pride. "Yes," Sabrina said to Oliver. "They fit you very well. Oliver, let me present my – ur – friend, Mindy."

Oliver nodded in acknowledgement. "Very pleased to make your acquaintance."

Mindy recovered herself. "Yes, me too." She stared at Sabrina, willing her to explain who Oliver was in her life.

Sabrina hesitated. "Oliver is my uh – uh —"

"Husband," Oliver said.

"Boyfriend," Sabrina said at the same time.

Mindy looked from one to the other, perplexed.

"Oh, Oliver." Sabrina gave him a wide smile. "Always joking. That's what it is, a joke." She laid a hand on his arm. "We've been together so long that we feel like an old married couple. Good seeing you."

Mindy reluctantly took the hint. After she left, Oliver turned to Sabrina, "What is a boyfriend?"

Sabrina could not mistake the edge in his voice. "It's like a husband. Same meaning actually, just a different word." Sabrina hoped her facial expressions hadn't given away the lie. She was a very poor liar.

Oliver eyed her skeptically. "If that is so, why would not husband do just as well?"

"It would if it didn't make us seem so old." Sabrina felt herself warming up to the explanation. "You see, in this time, persons of our age do not call each other husband and wife. That is for people who are forty or fifty. People in their twenties call each other boyfriend and girlfriend. So that is why I told Mindy it was a joke, because *husband* isn't the right word."

"But they both mean that you and I are married?"

Sabrina nodded.

Oliver grabbed her hand and kissed it. "Good. I don't think I could let you go."

Sabrina blushed furiously and shooed him back into the dressing room in order to compose herself. When Oliver re-emerged, she helped him select two pairs of jeans, the dark-wash and the hipster-skinny and four tee shirts, including the blue one and then, after a stop by the men's underwear to get him enough to last a week, plus a few pairs of socks, they progressed to men's shoes. They were fortunate to find a pair of black Chuck Taylor knock offs that had been discounted twice and now sat on the fifty percent off clearance. This meant that Sabrina would be out less than $150 for the whole thing; a bargain really when she thought of how good Oliver had looked in the clothes.

It was only in the line to pay that Sabrina wondered at the wisdom of buying clothes for a complete stranger, who was looney enough to think he was her husband. She had to be nuts. Then again, Oliver was beginning feel less like a stranger, particularly since he confirmed perfectly to the description of her favorite literary hero. And how could she account for his obvious innocence with regard to modern technology? It was a puzzle. She looked back at

Oliver, who was raptly contemplating the sales associate working the register. A real puzzle.

When they got to the front of the line, Oliver placed the clothing on the counter and said. "Your machine is marvelously strange, how does it work?"

The associate looked at him. She was a mousey girl with long stringy hair and flat skin. Her eyes had the blank look of a deer in headlights. "Uh, what machine?"

Oliver indicated the register. She shrugged her shoulders. "I don't know." She quickly swiped the tags. "That'll be $148.52."

Sabrina handed her a credit card.

"Credit or debit?"

"Credit, but it's one of those ones with a chip," Sabrina said.

"Oh." The associate jammed it into the machine.

"Just how much is $148.52 equivalent to in guineas?" Oliver said.

"At about two dollars a pound, it's roughly seventy."

"Seventy!" His mouth dropped open. "Seventy pounds!"

The associate looked at Oliver and then Sabrina. "Ignore him. He's just excited at how inexpensive everything is in America," Sabrina said.

The associate nodded and then gave the receipt to Sabrina to sign, while she stuffed the purchases in a plastic bag and pushed them a cross the counter.

Sabrina refused to answer any of Oliver's questions until she'd hustled him out of the store and into a coffee shop. "There has been quite a lot of inflation in two hundred years. Things don't cost what they did."

"At least you gave her that card instead of coins."

"It is a credit card, and it works like a letter from a bank would. The bank then sends the money to the store," Sabrina replied.

"There are no coins or banknotes anymore?"

"Yes there are. We use both now." Sabrina opened her wallet and handed Oliver a dollar bill. Then she fished around and handed him a penny.

He stared at the dollar. "George Washington? I still cannot imagine him as a heroic figure. He is a traitor to his country."

"Don't say that too loud," Sabrina replied. "Here, look at this. This is Abraham Lincoln;the president who ended slavery in the United States."

"How fortunate. The slave trade is a vile and inhuman enterprise." He studied the penny. "2010. I still cannot believe my eyes. To think I should live to see this day."

"Are you two going to order?" The guy behind the counter said sullenly.

"Yes." Sabrina squinted up at the board.

"What are all of these beverages?" Oliver said. "Do Americans also now speak the Italian tongue?"

"It's just coffee. The Italian is added to make it sound elegant. Do you take your coffee black or with milk? Or milk and sugar?"

"I'll have whatever you suggest."

She ordered two lattes and then went down the line to pay for them. As she dug out her wallet, her cell phone rang.

"Dave! Where have you been?" Sabrina tucked the phone onto her shoulder and paid the bill through a series of mimed gestures.

"Hay Sab, you'll never guess. They asked us to stay on for another night!"

"That's great, but did you listen to any of the voicemails I left you?"

"Yeah, but I don't know what you're talking about. I got a few actor friends but none of them are in Chicago right now. Oh and hey, I'm sending you the $200 bucks I owe you."

"That should come in handy. And you're sure you're not pulling some prank? Be straight with me."

"I'm not, honest! I mean, if you have guys sneaking into your apartment, that's your deal. TMI Sab," Dave said.

"Okay. Thanks I guess, and it's not, Sab."

Dave laughed and hung up. Sabrina looked at Oliver who was staring in rapped attention at the cell phone. At least that probably meant he hadn't been paying much attention to the conversation.

"What new miracle is that box in your hand?" Oliver said.

"It's a long story. Let's go get our coffees. I just heard them call our order."

They spent the next hour talking about the invention of telephones and computers. Then Sabrina showed Oliver the camera function and they were off again on photography and the physics of light. It had been a long time since Sabrina had had a conversation with anyone about such nerdy subjects, and she was kind of enjoying not hiding her intelligence under a barrel. Whoever Oliver actually was, he didn't bore her.

When they got back to the apartment, Sabrina pulled out her laptop. The computer was the one present her parents had ever given her that was truly useful. She opened it and pulled up the Internet. This engendered another hour explaining how a series of interconnected computers could span the globe and a detailed demonstration of the functions of both the keyboard and the mouse. Oliver was enthralled with all of these inventions. Sabrina left him happily Googling things with one-finger typing while she dug around the kitchen for some peanut butter and jelly to make sandwiches for a late lunch.

Although Dave could be taking the joke too far by lying to her, Dave's call had unsettled Sabrina. If Dave hadn't sent him, then where did Oliver come from? Did her bedroom contain some portal to the past? Just the thought of her dingy bedroom as the location for a rift in time made Sabrina laugh. But if it were true, then why did he have the name and the physical characteristics of the hero of her favorite novel? It didn't make sense. Nothing made sense. Maybe she should let him stay until the truth revealed itself. Oliver certainly didn't seem in a hurry to leave just yet.

Sabrina heard Oliver's musical laughter and made a final decision. She would go along with it, act the part of the girlfriend for as long as it took to get some answers. She thought about how good Oliver had looked in his jeans.

What could be the harm in that?

Chapter 5

Sabrina left the apartment early on Monday morning with a note for Oliver on the kitchen counter explaining that she would be back in the evening. She got in to work before most of her coworkers, but not before Giles. Through the glass panels of his office, she could tell that he was hunched at his desk, staring at his computer screen. Sabrina slouched a little lower in her cube.

Unfortunately, slumping didn't seem to work. Sabrina heard Giles' door open behind her. "Sabrina?" She loved the way his voice caressed her name.

"Yes?" she replied.

"I need your help with something."

Sabrina hurried over, trying not to trip over her feet. Once inside the door, Giles gestured at her to come around behind his desk. Then he pointed at his computer screen. "What do you make of that?"

Sabrina squinted at the row of numbers on the screen, acutely aware of the incredible smell of Giles' cologne. It was something dark and spicy. Probably European. Certainly nothing she'd ever smelled on any of the college guys she'd ever gotten drunk enough to get close to. "Are those sales figures?" she said.

"Yes, by region. Now, wouldn't it make sense that our sales should be highest in the regions where there are the largest numbers of farms?"

"But our sales are highest in New York?" Sabrina said.

"Exactly. What is happening in the other regions? Shouldn't we have higher sales in the Midwest?"

"I don't know."

"Well then, we must find out. There is a big trade show in two months, and I want to preview a new ad campaign. But I won't know where to go unless we figure out why we aren't selling well in the biggest markets."

"Do you mean Farm Con?" Sabrina had only heard about this bacchanalia of all things farm culture – going to Farm Con was like winning the lottery around the Federal offices. The expense accounts were unlimited. Her boss had been once when they needed someone in a pinch, but otherwise only the very top people at the company were allowed to go.

"Yes, Farm Con. And if you can help me figure out what that campaign will look like, I'll take you with me."

Sabrina stood in stunned silence for a moment and then said, "But won't an ad campaign take more than two months to put together?"

He smiled at her and she felt her knees go all wobbly. Seriously, Sabrina. You need to get a grip.

"Want to see what our ad agency produced for us already?" His eyes twinkled.

"More models on tractors?"

The smile turned to a grin as he pulled an image up – a very hot guy was seated atop a Federal tractor. His muscles rippled under his tight plaid shirt, which was unbuttoned just enough to catch a glimpse of glistening flesh. His hand was raised, wiping the sweat from his brow. The gesture accentuated the firm swell of his biceps under the fabric. Sabrina had to admit that if she were Federal's targeted demographic, she would run right out and buy a tractor. Maybe two.

She felt Giles' eyes upon her and looked away from the screen. She could feel her cheeks getting warm. "That is quite an eyeful," she said to say something.

"I think we agree on that. The problem is what to replace it with?"

"I don't know."

There was a knock on the door and Marilyn stalked in, dressed in a black 1980's-style power suit with big lumpy shoulders and bright red lapels. Her hair had been pulled up on her head and plied with enough hairspray to make the beehive concoction impenetrable.

"Sabrina, I want you in my office immediately," Marilyn said.

"Oh okay." Sabrina quickly moved out from behind the desk.

"Just a minute," Giles said. "Sabrina and I were still talking."

Marilyn folded her arms across her massive chest. "Look, I don't know what you mean by talking to one of the employees in my department, but if you think you can just waltz into Federal and take over, you are fooling yourself."

Giles stood up. Marilyn was a big woman, but Giles still had enough height to look down on her. "I think you may have forgotten that you report to me? And if I want to have Sabrina help me out with a special project, I will take as much of her time as I need."

Marilyn's beady little eyes narrowed. "I'm not sure what this special project is except an opportunity for you two to make googly eyes at each other on work time." She turned to Sabrina. "You should be ashamed of yourself, carrying on like this. What would your boyfriend have to say about this?"

"My boyfriend?"

"Mindy said you had one, although by the looks of you I'm really not seeing it. And you." She turned on Giles. "If you think I won't go to Human Resources if you so much as lay a hand on her, you can think again. Federal is a good family company and won't tolerate any sort of foreign shenanigans."

Marilyn took Sabrina by the arm and pushed her forward. "Back to your desk." Sabrina hurried out the door.

When the door was shut behind Sabrina, Giles said to Marilyn, "That was completely uncalled for and won't be tolerated again." He was so angry that he had to force his hands to stay at his side and not wrap themselves around Marilyn's large ropey neck. But cool control had always been his hallmark, and he wasn't about to change now.

"Just try me," Marilyn spat back. "I don't care who you think you are, but I know the board doesn't trust you. They've given you six months to turn things around or you'll be out on your boney French behind."

Giles gritted his teeth but remained calm. "Belgian. I am from Belgium. And how do you know what the board wants?"

Marilyn smiled like a cat that had just eaten the canary. "My uncle is Chairman of the Board. So don't get any ideas about trying to have me fired either. I have survived ten Vice Presidents of Marketing and I will survive you too."

And with that, Marilyn flounced out of the office. Giles sat down and stared at the computer, willing his body to relax. He had dealt with people like Marilyn before. He just had to work smarter. From now on, he would talk to Sabrina alone, away from the office. He needed to find a way to turn things around so that even the Board couldn't stop him, and then he would crush Marilyn like a bug beneath his shoe. So that last part wasn't good, but he didn't care. Sabrina might know how it could be accomplished. She seemed in some undefinable way to be working on his wavelength – certainly better than his current team. As soon as he had a sense of where to go with the advertising campaign, he would bring on the ad agency that he had worked with for Legends.

He looked at the image of the model on the tractor. It was so bad it could have been the cover of a porn movie. Darren Does Dakota. More likely gay porn. Darren Does – wait, was there a state that sounded like a man's name? No, better to go with a city or something. Darren Does Deadwood had a nice ring to it besides the double meaning. Sabrina would certainly blush at that one.

Sabrina. Sabrina had a boyfriend. Giles wasn't sure why he cared. He hadn't ever thought of her in any way even remotely like that – except it shifted his perception of her in some subtle fashion. Another man had seen something beneath those ugly glasses and shapeless dresses. And Sabrina wasn't going home to an empty apartment like he was. She had someone. He thought about Helene and felt a stabbing pain deep down in his gut. He had to get over Helene.

Sabrina stumbled back to her cube and met a torrent of questions from the prairie dog cubemates around her. When she'd successfully fended off questions about Giles and his interest in her and about what, if anything, Marilyn had said to her, she rounded on Mindy. "Why did you tell Marilyn I had a boyfriend?"

"I ran into her next day after I ran into you. Why? Don't tell me you have a problem with that? I mean, you told me you and Oliver had been together a long time."

"Yes, but I don't really want Marilyn of all people knowing all about my love life."

The heads above the cube walls nodded in agreement.

Mindy looked at her cubemates. "You guys wouldn't think that if you got a look at her boyfriend. I swear, if I had a guy that hot, I would be showing him off all over town."

There was a general murmur of excitement and several requests to see a picture. Sabrina felt her cheeks flush, but reluctantly produced her phone and pulled up a couple of shots of Oliver in his new jeans. This was followed by demands to know if he had any brothers. cousins, second cousins, friends or any other single guy connections that might be tapped for dates.

The hubbub finally quieted down when Marilyn stalked through the area on her way to lunch. Sabrina unearthed her usual peanut butter and jelly sandwich and had just taken a bite, when Becky called her. "You are coming to lunch today with me and we are going to talk. I am seriously upset, but I'll buy you lunch anyway because I know that that's the only way you'll come."

"Thanks for the offer, but what have I done now?"

"Don't try to deny anything, just meet me in front in ten minutes."

Becky was already waiting when Sabrina arrived. Becky was a heavyset middle-aged woman with dark hair that had gone gray in patches. She was dressed in a faded black skirt that hung around the thickest part of her calves and a stretchy gray top that did nothing to either restrain or enhance her abundant figure. Both garments were liberally doused with cat hair. Her feet were stuffed into scuffed black flats that had needed a polish several years ago, but now, with the help of street dust, had turned an indeterminate gray color.

But what Becky lacked in style, she generally made up in kindness to her five cats and the many humans who called Becky a friend. She certainly had been one to Sabrina ever since Sabrina had joined Federal Farm Machinery. In fact, if Sabrina discounted a couple of college friends who were too busy to get together much, Becky was probably Sabrina's best friend. They had certainly shared many a single-girl night on the town, which for them usually meant pizza and a movie at one of their apartments, enjoyed with a glass of boxed wine in a nod to the Sex and the City ideals they had hopelessly failed to live up to.

"Okay, so when were you going to tell me about the boyfriend?" Becky said as they turned by tacit agreement in the direction of a hole-in-the-wall sandwich shop two blocks away.

"Seriously Becky, I wasn't holding out on you, I swear. I mean, he just showed up."

"Then why is everyone buzzing about this man who you said you'd been dating for a long time?"

"Everyone is buzzing about my love life? Even over in Finance?"

"It was a slow day for gossip," Becky admitted. "Still, I would think as your friend I would have heard the news before Larry, the copier guy."

"Larry is talking about me, now? Geez."

86

"So, what is the story? And why am I just now hearing about it?"

"Because it just happened. Like, I met him last week." Sabrina bit her lip, trying to think up a probable story. "He's a friend of Dave's who is in town and needed a place to crash for a while. I hadn't met him before, but I figured that I'd help him out, being Dave's friend and all. So when he showed up, we really hit it off. But then we ran into Mindy while shopping for clothes, and she seemed so shocked that I was with him, that I told her we'd been together forever. Oliver, that's his name, played along because he's a good sport. So there you have it."

They reached the shop and Becky pulled the door open. Sabrina walked in, feeling Becky's skeptical eyes on her back. However, Becky didn't say anything more until they'd gotten their sandwiches and squeezed into a rickety table.

"Do you have a picture of this Oliver?" Becky said. "Because the scuttlebutt is that he is gorgeous, but, if you'll forgive the inference, I found that part a little hard to believe."

Sabrina pulled out her phone and showed Becky the pictures of Oliver in jeans. Becky sucked in her breath sharply.

"Seriously Sabrina. He is delicious," she said.

Sabrina smiled sheepishly. "He is, isn't he. But nothing has happened yet – I'm not the kind of girl."

"If I were you, I'd eat him up. Yum."

"He's not a dinner."

"Well, I'd make a move before someone else snatches him."

"What has gotten into you? I thought you didn't think men were worth the trouble?" Sabrina said.

"The men I run into aren't worth the trouble. In my age group, they've all gone to seed. If I could do the cougar thing, however, I might reconsider."

Sabrina nodded.

"And I hear that Oliver is not the only man of interest. Someone told me that Marilyn blew a gasket because Giles Philippe has been showing you a little too much attention."

"I'm not sure why, but he told me that he wants me to help him develop a new ad campaign to present at Farm Con."

"Ooo, that's big."

"It's big, but I don't bring anything to the table other than common sense," Sabrina replied.

"Maybe common sense is missing from the Marketing Department."

"If you look at the last couple of ad campaigns, I think it has been."

"I liked the last ad campaign," Becky said.

"You are not our demographic."

"Agreed. So what do you plan to do?"

"I don't know." And then Sabrina's phone rang. She looked at the number but didn't recognize it. "Hello? Mr. Philippe? Um, yes, I mean Giles. No, I'm just grabbing lunch. Hold on a minute." Sabrina stood up and gestured at Becky that she was going outside to have a private conversation. Becky looked disappointed.

When Sabrina reached the street she said, "I'm sorry but I couldn't hear you very well in there."

"Where are you?" Giles said.

"Bob's Deli, but I can come back to the office if you need me to."

"No, I'll come to you. I've been looking at the sales results for New York and something strange is showing up in the data. I'd like your thoughts, but given Marilyn's fit of temper, I would prefer not to call you into my office again."

"Oh, of course, but I'm having lunch with Becky Lorman, from Finance."

"Fine. Maybe she can help us as well. I'll be there in two minutes."

Giles hung up and Sabrina rushed back into the restaurant. "Becky, you are never going to believe this. Giles is coming here to talk to us. Something about sales in New York. Do you know anything in particular about our New York sales other than that we seem to be doing well there?"

Becky looked like someone had bonked her on the head. Hard. "Giles Philippe is coming to Bob's Deli to talk to us?"

"Yes, but he's not that scary in person, I promise," Sabrina said. Although, who was she kidding? Giles scared the bejezus out of her. She had yet to have any conversation with him where she did not feel like the most awkward human on the planet.

Becky absently took a bite of sandwich, but her eyes still seemed unfocused. "Sappho Farms," she said suddenly.

"What?"

"That's our biggest client in terms of sales. In New York, I mean. It's in upstate, a couple of hours outside of New York City."

And then Sabrina heard the door clank open. She turned her head and caught sight of Giles. He smiled at her and she felt a rush of adrenaline so intense that her head hurt. She blinked and blinked again, hoping to get her head back into some good order. It was vitally important that she maintain a clear head.

Giles reached the table in several long strides. "Ms. March and Ms. Lorman. Thank you so much for giving me bit of your lunch hour."

Becky recovered first. "Sure. What did you want to speak with us about, Mr. Philippe?"

He sat down in a rickety chair. "Call me Giles, please. And I need some clear thinking."

That was unfortunate, thought Sabrina, but she pasted on a smile. "We'll do our best."

Giles turned that megawatt smile of his on the pair of them and Sabrina heard Becky's quick intake of breath. It had clearly been a long time since Becky had been the recipient of that kind of smile. Sabrina steeled herself. Business. Clear head. Her thoughts must be reined in and channeled toward the work ahead.

"As I told Sabrina earlier, I've been looking at the sales figures and trying to tie them back to our marketing, and the figures just don't add up. We are strongest in the state of New York, not where one would expect in the Midwest or West given the concentration of agricultural land and our targeted marketing. Our largest client this year was —"

Becky seemed to be in a Giles-induced stupor, and so Sabrina stole her line. "Sappho Farms. They had the largest number of purchases, which must mean that they are expanding, because I can't imagine most farms, even large ones, purchasing so many expensive machines."

Giles smiled. "I talked to the salesman in charge of that region and he told me that they were indeed expanding. Or should I say incorporating. Sappho Farms is now one of the largest organic cooperatives in the country."

Becky recovered enough to add, "I assume that the Sappho in the name is deliberate?"

"Yes," Giles replied. "It is run by a lesbian couple, Anne and Marci Hammer-Smith."

"So did the salesman know why they bought equipment from us? If they are a lesbian couple, they probably didn't respond all that well to the male model on a tractor advertising theme."

"He didn't know, but I think that we need to know why if we want to design the right sort of marketing. That's why we are going there this weekend," Giles said.

"We?" Sabrina said.

"You and me. I have an appointment with the Hammer-Smith's lined up for Sunday afternoon."

Sabrina blinked. "But why me?"

"You have something I don't."

Sabrina wondered if he was going to say what she was thinking.

"You're relatable. I may be stereotyping, but I don't think that the Hammer-Smiths are going to instantly warm to a city man with a Belgian accent. You on the other hand have that American woman sort of easy demeanor. They can't help but like you."

Sabrina wasn't sure she really liked the idea of Giles assuming that she would appeal to a lesbian couple, however down to earth they turned out to be. "Well I guess, but —"

"No hesitation. I've booked our flights. We fly into LaGuardia on Saturday night, and I got rooms at my favorite hotel. They have a fantastic steakhouse. Anyway, I'll send you the e-ticket and you can meet me at the airport. Or better yet, I'll pick you up."

Sabrina had a mental image of the elegant Giles in her cramped tatty apartment, meeting Oliver. No! He could certainly not meet Oliver. Sabrina wasn't sure what a 19th Century man, or a man who pretended to be one, would think of his wife going off alone on a business trip with another man, but she didn't want to find out. Besides, one sentence into a conversation, Giles was sure to discover that Oliver was different. And even if he didn't keep up his Regency boyfriend act, she wasn't sure she wanted Giles to know about the lengths her brother and his friends went for a practical joke.

"I'll meet you at the airport."

"Thank you," he replied. Although it was clear that he'd had no doubt about her response. Sabrina felt the stirring of annoyance. She shouldn't be this easy to bulldoze.

Giles turned to Becky. "I know I can rely on your discretion. Marilyn will be very angry about my robbing her department's best employee."

Sabrina started to say that Marilyn hadn't exactly objected because Sabrina was her prized employee, but Becky replied loyally, "You have my word. I know what kind of work Sabrina is capable of. You couldn't have picked a better person to take with you to Sappho Farms."

After dutifully paying their bill, Giles left them to digest his sudden appearance in peace.

Becky said, "You and Oliver aren't exclusive are you? I'd take full advantage of a weekend trip with Mr. Philippe. He is – wow. That's all I'm going to say."

"No, but Giles would never be interested in me." And then the truth hit her like a ton of bricks. Oliver. If he was really a man from the past, how was she supposed to leave him alone for two days? He wouldn't know what to do without her. It was crazy. Becky would never believe such a half-cocked story, but Sabrina did not have any good answers. She would just have to be honest with Becky and let the chips fall where they may. "Becky, I can't explain it all right now, because we need to get back, but can you come home with me? I want you to meet Oliver."

"He's still living with you?"

"It's very complicated. And promise you won't judge until you've met him."

"Won't judge? What is going on with you?" Becky

said.

"Some days I don't know myself."

Chapter 6

On the way to her apartment that evening,

Sabrina made a clean breast of the situation

with Oliver.

Becky shook her head. "Letting a mentally ill guy

stay with you and pretend to be your boyfriend doesn't

sound like the best idea I've ever heard."

"I know, but the weird thing is that I don't think he

is mentally ill. I mean, when you talk to him, he seems

perfectly normal."

"Except that he believes he is an earl from some

trashy romance novel and that you are his wife."

"Girlfriend," Sabrina replied.

"He thinks it is the same thing."

"Right, but how did he get in my apartment?

Everything was still locked when I got up that morning."

"Maybe he's an actor friend of your brother's like you initially thought. He'll leave once your brother tells him to."

"But he has never once broken character. And why would he stay when the jig is up? I already confronted Dave about it."

They reached her building and climbed the stairs. When they got to her door, however, they stopped. The door was unlocked. Sabrina opened it cautiously, "Oliver? Are you there?" There was no reply. Sabrina felt her heart speed up a tick. "Oliver? Seriously, this is not funny."

Becky pushed past her into the apartment. "He's not here. No one is here."

"Oh my God, what could have happened?"

Becky walked over to the table by the kitchen area. "He left a note, but I'll be damned if I can read it. What kind of cursive is this?"

Sabrina grabbed the note out of her hand. "It is how they wrote back then. The *S* looks like a *F* and so forth."

"How do you know that stuff?"

"I am obsessed with Regency romances, remember?" Sabrina stared at the note. "He says he went out and will be back soon. But where could he have gone? He doesn't know how to drive or use mass transit – at least I don't think he does – assuming he's not an actor or a mental patient. We have to go look for him."

"Why? He's an adult. Won't he be able to find his way back?" Becky said.

"Then stay here. That's better anyway, in case he comes back. I'll call you. Just make yourself at home." And with that, Sabrina dashed out the door.

Giles sat at his desk, contemplating the square buttons of his office phone. Good thing he still knew Jerome at the steakhouse and could swing a reservation for

two at such short notice. Jerome had hinted around, trying
to see if Giles had some new woman he was bringing to
town, but Giles merely laughed it off. If only he did have
some new woman – a woman as jaw-droppingly-beautiful
as Helene. One who turned heads the moment she walked
in the room. One as lean and cool as Helene. Helene could
give you a look from those gray eyes of hers that would
freeze your veins and melt your bones at the same time. It
sent a shiver of desire down his spine just thinking about it.
God, how he missed her.

Giles turned back to his computer. Work. He had
to work. He thought about his meeting with Sabrina and
Becky and smiled. If he had to go to the wilds of New
York, Sabrina would at least be up to the challenge. And
she was someone to talk to. Giles realized with a pang that,
outside of work, he had no human contact of any kind.
Maybe he should get a cat.

Sabrina walked down three blocks in one direction, calling Oliver's name, but he didn't respond and people were starting to look at her as if she were deranged. Where could Oliver have gone? Sabrina finally understood what Becky went through every time one of her cats got loose. But seriously, this was worse than having a lost pet. She turned around and started to walk the other direction. It was when she'd passed her apartment building and gone two blocks that she saw the coffee shop on the corner. Could he have gone there? She started to run.

She pulled open the door and a wave of air-conditioned air, fragrant with the smell of fresh coffee and pastry dough, hit her in the face. She realized that she was ravenously hungry. All the excitement around Giles had taken away her appetite at lunch. Please, she thought, please let Oliver be here so that I can get home and eat. And there was Oliver, standing at the bar right in front of the coffee machines, sipping coffee and deep in conversation with the barista. Praying did work!

"Oliver!" Every head turned to see who the raving lunatic was at the door. Sabrina approached Oliver and said in a softer tone, "What are you doing?"

"Ah my love, I have spent the most fascinating hour speaking with Mr. Jones about how this wondrous coffee machine works. Did you know that water flows right into it via a metal tube? And that the water is filtered to remove impurities? And that the machine even has settings for the grinding of coffee beans? And the steam – you should come and see the steam!"

Sabrina looked over at the barista who gave her a harried look that clearly indicated how much of a pest Oliver had made himself through his probing questions. "It is quite a miracle, I know. But, please come back with me. I want to introduce you to my friend Becky."

"Of course my dear," Oliver replied.

The barista shot Sabrina a grateful look. Sabrina grabbed Oliver's hand and pulled him out to the street. "Please don't wander off again Oliver! The city is not safe if you don't know where you are going."

"I have an excellent sense of direction, dear wife. Always have. And you know that the coins of these United States are very easy to understand. I made a study of the ones in the dish in the kitchen. Every coin is based on the number ten!"

"I'm sure you do have an excellent sense of direction, but many things have changed. You can't just leave the apartment." Then she hesitated. He was an adult after all. "Please, for my sake, you must let me know where you are going. And I will give you a key. It's not a good idea to leave the apartment unlocked."

Oliver lifted her hand his to his lips and gave her a look full of promise and longing. "For your sake, anything."

Sabrina blushed up to the roots of her hair. "Um, thanks. Let's go. Becky is waiting for us."

Becky had taken the make-yourself-at-home instruction literally and when they walked in the door, she was dumping a tin of tuna in a casserole dish. "Tuna casserole was the only thing I could come up with given what you have in your cupboards. You don't eat very well do you?" she said.

"I'm a Junior Copywriter straight out of college. I think I'm doing as well as you can expect." And then turning to Oliver, Sabrina added, "This is Becky. Becky, let me introduce you to Oliver, or should I say, the Earl of March."

Oliver inclined his head, but Becky, entering into the spirit of the thing, curtsied low. "Rebecca Lorman, enchanted milord."

Oliver smiled. "Miss Lorman. It is lovely to meet any friends of Sabrina."

Sabrina turned to Oliver. "I wanted you to meet Becky because I will have to go away on a business trip this Saturday and won't be back until late Sunday. Becky will be stopping by to check in on you while I am gone because I know that this world is new yet, and you might need some assistance."

"Business?" he said, seemingly stricken. "What business is this that can take you away from me?"

"You know that in this time, women, even titled women, have some sort of employment besides child rearing and managing the house. I go away every day to a job at Federal Farm Machinery, where I write things about tractors to put on the Internet. The Internet is that magical screen that you use to search for information on my computer. Our tractors haven't sold well. I need to visit a farm where they bought our tractors so that we can know what sells."

"And where is this farm?"

"In New York State. That was one of the colonies. Maybe you remember? It is on the East Coast."

"I do remember, but how will you go so far and return the next day? It is impossible even with the horseless carriages I have seen."

"I will fly," Sabrina replied.

"Like the birds? Surely you jest!"

"It is called an airplane." Sabrina went over and opened her laptop. She pulled up a picture of a jet airplane. "See? They have gasoline engines that push down so hard that the plane and all of the people inside it go up. Here." She found a video of a plane taking off.

Oliver stood with his mouth open. "That cannot be!"

"It can be. Search the Internet yourself. It's called an airplane." She set the laptop on the card table and pulled out a chair for him. He eagerly sat and stared at the screen, completely absorbed by the concept.

Sabrina sidled over to Becky, who was sprinkling grated cheese on top of the casserole. "So what's your take?" she said in a low voice.

"Boy, I'm having a hard time thinking he is anything but a 200 year old guy. Did you see his expression when you talked about the plane? I could have sworn he'd never heard of them before."

Sabrina smiled. "I want to look that young at 200. Do you think he's a vampire?"

"That's probably more likely than he's a character out of a novel come to life. You might want to stock up on the garlic," Becky replied.

"So what should I do?"

Becky looked over at Oliver, who was gleefully Googling. "I don't know. Watch him for a bit. I mean, he seems harmless enough, but you never know."

"Most serial killers don't pretend to be from the 1800's in order to gain your trust."

"And you are sure he's not a friend of Dave's?" Becky said.

"Dave swears he isn't, but that is the only explanation I can come up with that makes any sense."

"At least he's easy on the eyes. And he really seems to like you."

"That's just because he mistakes me for someone else."

"I don't think there is much mistaking how he looks at you," Becky said.

"Hmm," Sabrina replied, anxious to move off the topic. "So you'll come by a check in on him?"

"Sure. I've got nothing better to do this weekend." Becky slid the casserole in the oven and closed the oven door. "Your oven looks pristine."

"I don't use it much," Sabrina admitted.

"What have you been feeding the Earl of March?"

"Spaghetti and sandwiches mostly."

"He likes that?"

"Compared to Regency food anything out of a jar is an improvement. It isn't spoiled and it doesn't have vermin in it. He thinks I'm a miracle worker."

"Then he is going to love me." Becky set the oven timer. "You might just have to find yourself another boyfriend when I'm done."

Sabrina laughed.

Chapter 7

But she wasn't laughing early Saturday morning as she stuffed the best of her dresses into a carry-on. She was running late because she'd spent too much time looking for the one bra that didn't make her look saggy in that particular dress. She eventually located the bra, wedged between the end of a drawer and the back of the dresser, but the search had cost her valuable time. Although, what did it really matter anyway? She felt dowdy enough in Chicago, let alone New York, and let alone in New York with someone like Giles. As she threw a set of black heels she could just barely walk in into the case, she caught sight of her grandmother's pendant, half hidden by *To Kiss an Earl*. She grabbed it and clasped it around her neck. The necklace would dress up her outfit a little.

Oliver offered to help, but there wasn't much he could do other than listen as Sabrina rattled off instructions about the apartment and the building and the neighborhood. He nodded solemnly. Then, as she was about to leave, Oliver said, "I know I have agreed to act the part of a gentleman, but I must beg of you a kiss sweet Sabrina before you leave me. For I do not trust that I shall see you again ere long."

Sabrina stopped in her tracks, considering the matter. What was one little kiss? "Oh, well, if you think you must."

Oliver took her hand and pulled her to him. Sabrina found herself putting her hands around his neck. He leaned down and very gently pressed his lips to hers. It was a sweet kiss, a delicate kiss – a kiss that might have gone somewhere, but didn't. She could feel how Oliver held back with her, as if any sign of passion might frighten her away. The consideration touched Sabrina. He was sweet,

114

whoever he was, but in some way she couldn't define, too perfect. She pulled away and said, "Becky has a phone. I will call her to check on you. I won't be gone long, so don't worry."

"Just come back to me, my love," Oliver said.

Sabrina hurried out the door.

The flight to New York was uneventful. Giles seemed distracted and, in any case, they spent most of the time silently reviewing sales charts. Giles was in search of a marketing silver bullet, and Sabrina was trying to absorb enough data so that she wouldn't sound stupid when they finally talked. In the taxi ride to the hotel, which turned out to be one of those exclusive boutique hotels just outside the theater district, Giles finally made some remark not related to work, "Is this your first time to New York?"

"Does it show?"

Giles smiled. "No."

"I suppose that's a plus. After living in Chicago, I thought I could fake indifference, but I have to admit I'm as star struck as anyone. It's so much bigger and brighter than I thought it would be."

"I love New York," Giles said. "When I was doing Legends, I used to come here all of the time."

"You said that this was your favorite hotel?"

Giles nodded. "I always stayed here." He sighed in a way that indicated there was way more to the story, and then added wistfully, "In some ways it's good to be back."

Sabrina held her curiosity and continued to stare out the window. She felt tingly and just a little lightheaded from the energy that radiated from every atom of the city and the sensation of sitting, practically knee to knee, with Giles. Even as she focused her mind on the stores and the restaurants and the billboards, she was acutely aware of the heat of Giles' body, the rich smell of his cologne and the fact that they were cocooned together in the closed space of the cab.

When they got to the hotel, Sabrina realized that they would be sharing adjacent rooms, which wasn't surprising, but certainly didn't ease the sense of mysterious danger that had taken hold of her. This was New York and anything could happen. Not that it would happen, but the energy of the city made everything seem possible.

"We have reservations at seven o'clock since we'll have to get an early start tomorrow. They'll be bringing the car around tomorrow at six a.m. Why don't you meet me for drinks at the bar after you get settled in? Say at 6:15?" Giles said.

Sabrina nodded, and then had a moment of sheer panic. Nothing she had in her suitcase was chic enough for drinks in a hotel bar with someone as dashing and drool-worthy as Giles. But there was no time to get anything else,

117

so her best black dress would just have to do. And she would have those heels. As long as she was sitting no one would know that she couldn't walk in heels very well.

Sabrina's hotel room was small and precisely decorated to look antique and hip at the same time. The room boasted an even smaller bathroom done in various colors of marble. On the opposite wall, Sabrina noticed a door. This door led to the next room where Giles was presumably unpacking. Sabrina set her carry-on on the bed and pulled the black dress out to hang in the bathroom while she took a quick shower.

Giles frowned at his reflection in the bathroom mirror. What had gotten into him? He'd been grouchy and on edge since they'd taken off from Chicago. Sabrina must be tired of him already. And he shouldn't spoil her excitement at being in New York just because his memories had hit him like a ton of bricks as soon as they'd taken the cab to the hotel. Helene could not have such a hold on him still. Helene had certainly moved on. Giles simply had to forget her.

"I'll show Sabrina a good time at dinner," he mumbled to his reflection. It was the least he could do after dragging her with him on what could turn out to be a complete dead end. He heard the water go on in the room next door and the image of Helene, damp and glistening, emerging from the shower filled his brain. "Ugh!" This had to stop.

And this was Sabrina we were talking about, not Helene. His perverse brain tried the thought of Sabrina damp and glistening on for size, and found that it might not be bad. Sabrina had the kind of curves that probably looked ten times better without clothes on – particularly without those shapeless dresses she seemed to favor. And when would Sabrina realize that her glasses were too big for her face? She had pretty eyes if you could only see them. But he should not be thinking of Sabrina in that way or in any way. They were there for business. And he'd heard she had a boyfriend, so it would be useless. Besides, he'd vowed never to move in on another man's woman. It was un-gentlemanly for one and extremely messy for another. Giles hated messes. So why was he in such a mess now? Better not to think of it.

He shaved with ruthless precision and then changed into a clean shirt, grabbed his sport coat and headed for the bar. He was just starting a whisky and soda when Sabrina stumbled in. He jumped down from the bar stool and caught her arm before she toppled over. "Are you okay?"

She smiled ruefully, her cheeks flushed with embarrassment. "I'm afraid I don't do as well as I'd like with heels."

Giles looked down and realized that she had indeed traded her ballet flats for some very high black heels.

He had to admit that she had decent legs – more than decent. He resolutely pulled his eyes upwards to her face. "Your glasses!" he exclaimed.

She blinked at him with beautiful blue eyes. "I decided to put my contacts in. I don't wear them much but this is New York, so I brought them along just in case."

"Good idea," he replied lamely, because he didn't want to say anything more about her appearance. "Let me get you a drink." He held her elbow and gently guided her to the bar.

"What are you having?"

"Whisky and soda, but you can have anything you want."

Sabrina cocked her head to one side as if that would help her decide. "I'll try the same."

"Are you sure? You don't seem the whisky type."

"I'm not, but you only live once. It might be fun to live on the wild side for a change."

He signaled the bartender and ordered for Sabrina. Then he said, "Life as a – what was your title again?"

"Junior Copywriter."

"Life as a Junior Copywriter not exciting enough?"

"Not until lately. I like this hotel. I can see why you come here. It feels so out of the way, like a little hideaway in this big pulsing city."

Giles nodded. Sabrina had an uncanny way of getting to the truth of the matter. "They're very strict about the press or cameras or anything here, so famous people can come and not feel like the world is watching."

"How many famous people have you met here?"

Giles swallowed uncomfortably, but continued on, "Actors mostly. Robert DeNiro sat just where you are sitting. Over there at the end of the bar, I saw Oprah Winfrey."

Sabrina's eyes got big. "Oprah? What was she like?"

"Seemed nice enough. We didn't have much conversation."

"Wow." Sabrina's whisky arrived and she took a hesitant sip. "Not as bad as I feared."

"If you don't like it, I will order you something else."

"No. It has the kind of taste that grows on you."

She took longer sip and then looked at him over the rim of the glass. Giles was struck again at the beauty of her big blue eyes.

"Is this a popular drink in Belgium?" she said.

"Scottish whisky?"

Sabrina made a face. "I guess not. So what is a typical drink?"

"Beer. Belgians will drink beer with anything."

"Remind me to visit Belgium when I have the money."

"You like beer?" he said, surprised.

She nodded and then started him off on a long conversation about Belgian ales, followed by more discussion of Belgian food. By the time the hostess arrived to seat them at a small round table, a general discussion of the Belgian countryside ensued. As they perused their menus, Giles managed to mention cycling and that sent them off on another conversation about the Tour of Flanders and the Belgian Classics. Sabrina's combination of insightful questions and earnest attention was so potent that Giles found himself telling her all sorts of things he would never have imagined about his tastes and interests. He had to admit that it felt really good to talk to someone.

After they ordered, however, he put his foot down. "I have talked too much about myself. Now it's your turn."

"What do you want to know?" Sabrina had finished the whisky and was feeling pretty reckless – the way only strong alcohol and an empty stomach can make you. Her entire plan for this evening had been to get Giles to talk about himself so she wouldn't have to come up with other topics of conversation. So far, that strategy had worked like a charm. And really, Giles had done so many different things that it was a pleasure to hear him talk about them. Besides, his smooth voice slid over the words, the accent making every word sound delightfully decadent. Sabrina could listen to it for hours.

But now he wanted her to carry the conversation, and she really didn't have any ready material. She looked over his shoulder, hoping that something would come to her by way of distraction. And then, across the room, she saw the hostess appear with a gentleman in a dark suit and a tall indescribably elegant woman with pale skin and dark straight hair. No, it couldn't be – but yet it had to be.

"You were right about the celebrities. Isn't that the supermodel, Helene St. Just? And I could be wrong, but I think that's the actor Guy Lord with her!"

Giles turned quickly and then turned back, his face ashen.

"What's wrong?"

Giles grabbed Sabrina's hand across the table and squeezed it. "Please, just follow my lead and don't fight me."

"Fight you?"

"Yes, and don't tell Human Resources."

Before Sabrina could ask what he meant by that, he gave her a look so hot and scorching that Sabrina's cheeks instantly flushed crimson. Then he leaned over the table and firmly planted his lips on hers. That little voice in Sabrina's head that had always kept her from doing

anything remotely crazy screeched a frenzied *No! No! No!*
But Sabrina, in her devil-may-care whisky-induced New
York restless mood, decided to enjoy herself now and ask
painful questions later. Her other hand wrapped around his
neck and she kissed him back.

Oliver's kiss that morning notwithstanding, Sabrina
didn't have a large experience to go by, but even she, a
relative innocent in the sensual arts, could tell that Giles
knew what he was doing. His lips were soft and persuasive,
caressing hers. She felt the warm heat of desire flowing
through her veins and parted her lips ever so slightly. She
hadn't meant to do anything, but his tongue found hers. It
was like a match to a gallon of gasoline. Oh my God – how
she wanted him.

She felt his hand clench like a vice over hers at the
table and his free hand snake through her hair, the warmth
of his fingers on her neck and scalp. That was fine, but she

suddenly realized that she wanted those fingers everywhere. And just the thought of those strong gentle hands on her body made her kiss him more frenetically. She had to be dreaming. This couldn't be the real Sabrina March.

And then, all of a sudden, Giles pulled away and let go of her hand. Sabrina looked at him, confused and disoriented. His hair was tousled and his tie partially undone. He looked wild, his eyes wide in fear. "Did they see us?" he said.

"Who?"

"Helene St. Just and Guy Lord."

"How would I know? What is this all about?"

Giles looked in their direction. "They have seen us. And they're coming over. Please, bear with me a little longer and agree with everything I say."

Sabrina was about to answer, but Giles grabbed her hand again and squeezed it in warning. In any case, Helene and Guy arrived at the table. Guy was lean and muscular

128

with a megawatt smile the size of Texas and a seductive Southern drawl. These attributes had made him one of the most popular actors in the nation. Helene was beautiful in an angular way that the camera made unforgettable. Her hard gray eyes focused on Sabrina and Sabrina felt every blemish on her face and every extra pound on her body.

Guy stuck out his hand. "Giles. Good to see you again. What have you been doing with yourself since Legends? I kept hoping I'd get a call from my agent about a spectacular new Giles Philippe campaign."

Yes," Helene added. "You must call us you know, Giles. We'd love to work with you again." Her French accent swallowed the vowels with every breathy cadence. She pushed her long straight dark hair back with her hand, and Sabrina caught a glimpse of her engagement ring. It was even larger in person than it seemed on the pages of *People* magazine.

Gilles nodded. "I decided to take a little time off and do something different. I'm in Chicago now. Oh, sorry, let me introduce Sabrina March, my girlfriend." Giles turned to her. "Sabrina dear, this is Guy Lord and Helene St. Just. You remember, I told you that I worked with them on the Legends campaign."

Sabrina caught the pleading look in Giles' warm brown eyes and forced her mouth into a smile. "Yes, of course." She extended her hand and received a hearty shake from Guy and a cold squeeze from Helene's long fingers. "It's lovely to finally meet you. Giles has said so much. I know the campaign wouldn't have been nearly so successful without the two of you."

Guy smiled. "Thanks. What brings you all to New York?"

"We're just passing through," Giles said. "And you?"

Guy smiled at Helene. "Just a little wedding shopping between shoots. I'm working with Clint Eastwood on his next picture and we have some New York scenes. Filming starts tomorrow. You know how that is. Helene had some magazine work so we sneaked a day in between."

"When is the happy date?" Sabrina said.

"We haven't set it, yet," Helene replied. Her voice had a hint of coldness and Sabrina wondered if the date was ever going to be set. "Guy, we should leave Giles and Sabrina to their conversation."

"Sure. Good seeing you Giles. Nice to meet you Sabrina. You keep him in line, you hear?"

Sabrina smiled and ran her hand up Giles arm suggestively. "Not a problem. Have a good dinner."

When they were out of earshot, Giles said, "I don't know how I can ever repay you. You were absolutely amazing. Even I would have believed that we were a couple. You have no idea what it means to me."

Sabrina crossed her arms over her chest. "How about starting with giving me an explanation for the last ten minutes? And when did you date Helene St. Just? I spend too much time on the Internet, and I can tell you that your name has never been linked with her. Not even before Guy Lord put a ring on it."

Giles put his head in his hands and then, as if remembering that Helene and Guy might be watching, pasted a smile back on his face. "I owe you answers to anything you want to ask me, but please, can we wait till the wine arrives? I need another drink."

"I think you are in luck," Sabrina replied as their waiter appeared with a bottle of Malbec.

After taking a couple of large sips, Giles said, "Thanks again for being my pretend girlfriend. I just couldn't face Helene without having someone. She can't see me weak."

Sabrina took a sip of her wine. It wended its warm way down her throat and settled her nerves. "I assume you met her when she became the face of Legends?"

"I attended the screening and knew she was the one we were looking for. Guy was already on board and they had instant chemistry in front of the camera."

"Behind the camera as well, I read," Sabrina said.

"I didn't know that. Besides, Helene didn't want our relationship to go public. She said it would hurt the campaign. At the time, I thought she was right, but now I know that she was just ensuring that I never found out about Guy or he about me. Until she was sure of him and no longer needed me, that is."

Sabrina slowly drank her wine, digesting what he'd just said. "I'm sorry Giles, but you'll find someone else."

"I don't want someone else. That is the pathetic part."

"I see."

He smiled ruefully. "And now I've gone and thrown you in the middle. I am so so sorry." And then a thought seemed to strike him. "God, your boyfriend. I didn't even think about him."

"How do you know anything about my boyfriend?"

"Office gossip. What's his name, by the way?" Giles said.

"Oliver. Don't worry, I won't tell him about all this."

Giles breathed a sigh of relief. "I'm not sure what came over me, but when I saw her, I don't know. Something snapped."

"I get it," Sabrina said. But part of her wished she didn't, so that she could suspend disbelief for a little while and enjoy the memory of his lips on hers. Wow. And that was what a fake kiss from him felt like? Just imagine reality.

When the food arrived, Giles doggedly tried to get Sabrina to talk about herself. It was a welcome distraction from the thoughts that were swirling through his brain. It had to be the maddest most irrational evening he had ever spent, but that just went to prove how the relationship with Helene had warped him completely. He looked at Sabrina carefully cutting her steak into small pieces, purposely averting her gaze as she talked.

What must a woman like Sabrina think of him at this point? He could imagine the shock and outrage hidden beneath the expression of nonchalance she was trying to master. In her shoes, Giles would have slapped him at the first opportunity. He deserved it after grabbing her like that. Instead, she had put on a masterful act. Anyone, even the skeptical Helene, would believe that were really together after that kiss. Hell, he'd believed if for a minute or two until his rational brain asserted itself. No, there was way more to Sabrina March than Giles had originally expected.

After an hour of probing questions, Giles succeeded in getting a brief description of Sabrina's family and her thoughts on living in Chicago. She also mentioned that she hadn't really travelled at all but hoped to when she'd moved up the corporate ladder enough to command a better salary. Finally, her phone rang and she stepped away to take the call.

After ten minutes, she returned and sat down.

"I hope nothing's wrong," Giles said.

"No, that was just Oliver, wishing me a good night." A blush stole up Sabrina's cheek, making Giles think that she probably hadn't meant to say that.

"He is a very considerate boyfriend," Giles replied. Had Helene ever done that with him? Not that he could remember. Mostly her calls were brief directions on where to meet for some late night hook up. A pang of jealousy, coupled with remorse for kissing the poor man's beloved, made Giles feel a certain interest in Oliver, so he said, "What does he do for a living?"

"He's a – his family runs a farm, in England. He's British. But he just came over to visit for a bit."

"Really? I thought you said you hadn't travelled to Europe."

Sabrina took a deliberate sip of wine. "We met here. He's getting a Ph.D. in history and knew a friend of a friend of my brother so I met him through Dave. When Oliver came on a visit to Chicago, he uh stayed with me, you know, a student with no money. And so uh we started dating. Then we did the long-distance thing, but he's back now."

"How long is he staying?"

"I'm not sure. It depends on a bunch of things."

Giles resisted the urge to pry further. Sabrina's defiant look told him that for some reason Oliver was not Sabrina's favorite topic of conversation. He switched tactics. "Does Oliver have any experience with Federal tractors? I'd love to talk to him if he does. Our European sales are abysmal."

Sabrina started coughing over her wine.

"Are you okay?"

She nodded and then croaked out, "Wine went down the wrong way. Um, no. He doesn't have any experience with them."

"Too bad."

After dinner, Sabrina decided to beat a hasty retreat to her room. Giles showed no desire to linger either. "Remember, I'll be knocking on your door early tomorrow morning," he said when they reached the hallway outside their rooms.

"I'll be ready."

138

Giles turned to insert his card in the door and then turned back. "Thank you everything tonight. If you ever need anything, any favor, just ask. I know how much I owe you."

Sabrina flushed. "Good night, Giles. Sweet dreams."

Chapter 8

Ugh. Sabrina closed the door behind her in disgust. Sweet dreams? Could she sound any more lame? What on God's earth was the matter with her? Giles. That was the matter. She had the hots for him. The kiss had merely sealed the deal on the feelings that had been building up since he had arrived at Federal Farm Machinery. And he was in love with a supermodel! If that piece of information didn't just take the cake. As if Sabrina didn't need any more proof how out of his league she was. And yet he'd thought she'd be convincing as a substitute girlfriend. That was sort of flattering at least. However, Helene had probably seen right through the ruse. She didn't seem like a woman who missed much.

Sabrina struggled out of her dress and kicked off the hateful heels. She had to admit that she was tired. Bone tired. She took off her bra and then threw on an old stretched out tee shirt with Dave's band's logo on it. It had been a Christmas present from him, but Sabrina suspected that she'd gotten it because one of the bandmates ordered the wrong size. It hung down to mid-thigh on her. She brushed her teeth but couldn't drum up the energy to take off any of her makeup. One night couldn't hurt, could it? Her luck being what was, she would wake up tomorrow with a face full of zits.

Then again, what did it matter? Giles was off the table and Oliver seemed constitutionally blind to her faults. Oliver. She'd not told Giles the whole truth about the phone call. Oliver had wanted to wish her good night but really desired to call because Becky had told him about FaceTime and he had to try it out. And ask Sabrina a million questions about wifi and the properties of color and light, most of which she couldn't answer. She told him that they would Google together when she got back.

Sabrina climbed into bed and turned out the light. She lay there in the dark, trying not to think about Giles. She had work to do tomorrow and the best thing would be to keep up the front that the kiss hadn't meant anything to her. And really, if it didn't mean anything to him it shouldn't mean anything to her. She thought about Dave. She thought about the ocean. She thought about her bills and student loans. She thought about *Friends* and the chances of a reunion movie. She thought about anything but the feel of Giles' lips or the smell of his cologne and the heat of his fingers on her skin. Eventually, she drifted off into fitful sleep.

She awoke to the sound of knocking at the door. She sat up. It was still dark out and the shield of sleep befuddled her brain. She got out of bed and went to the room door and then realized that the knocking was coming from the door that connected the two rooms. What did Giles want now? Or maybe she'd overslept? Had she misjudged the time? She got the lock open.

"What do you want?" She stopped, her mouth half-open. Giles' eyes were heavy-lidded with that scorching look he'd worn at the table right before he kissed her. Sabrina felt the bones in her legs melt under her.

Giles didn't respond, but instead slid a hand around her waist and pulled her to him. The gesture was vaguely familiar, but Sabrina couldn't think clearly. He was only wearing a pair of silk boxers – a detail that seemed immensely foreign and seductive when it registered in some part of her addled brain. She reached a hand out and touched the smooth planes of his chest, feeling the sinewy muscle. His skin burned under her fingers and she realized that her skin also burned, exquisitely alive to every shift of his body against hers.

143

He tightened his grip and Sabrina now realized that the feeling of desire raging through her must be in some way reciprocated because he was hard against her body. He leaned his head down and Sabrina turned her face up, lost in the depths of his molten brown eyes. She must be dreaming, she thought, or in some sort of bad girl heaven.

And then his hungry look shifted. He shook his head as if to clear it. "Wait, what? Where am I?"

He let go of her waist and she stumbled backwards, nearly tripping over her own feet. The spell lifted. Sabrina glared at him. "In my room. Where do you think you are?"

"Your room? But, am I still dreaming?"

"No." Sabrina flushed crimson and crossed her arms in front of her chest. Her skin felt raw.

Giles ran his hand through his hair. "But I was —"

"You were what? What kind of game are you playing? In case you haven't noticed, Helene isn't here so there is no need to pretend."

"I know, but I was dreaming and —"

"You knocked on my door. Is this some sort of sleep walking thing?"

Although Sabrina had never heard of sleep sex, she supposed it might exist, especially given the deer in the headlights look Giles was giving her at the moment. He certainly didn't look like someone who knew what he was doing. Then again, he was a consummate actor if the performance for Helene had been any indication. Sabrina's anger flared to a fever pitch.

"Don't mess with me Giles. I'm done playing games so go back to your room and don't bother me again. Ever!"

Giles gave her a bewildered nod and closed the door behind him. Sabrina closed her door and resolutely turned the lock. She went to the bathroom and washed her face with cold water. Her watch on the counter told her that it was four o'clock in the morning. She might as well take a shower. It was while she was in the shower that Sabrina finally made the connection. She'd had a dream about Giles pulling her close and leaning down to kiss her. He'd been just about to when the knocks had startled her awake. Strange.

When she got out of the shower, she dressed in jeans and a loose top that could never be called seductive. She stood in front of the bathroom mirror to apply her makeup and realized that she was still wearing her grandmother's necklace. She must have slept in it by accident. She took it off so that it would not get damaged. Touring a farm didn't seem like the kind of activity that warranted good jewelry.

Giles flopped backwards on the bed and stared at the ceiling. What had gotten into him lately? One minute he was asleep and the next he was staring down into Sabrina's big blue eyes, wanting to kiss her more than anything in the world. Well, almost anything. He had to admit that the feel of her soft curves pressed against him made him think of doing a lot more than kissing her.

It was like he was in a trance or something. Sabrina wasn't even his usual type. His women tended to be like Helene, all angles and hard lines. And yet for some reason that seemed beyond his comprehension, he'd gotten out of bed to storm into her room and make love to her until she couldn't see straight. Only he was the one who couldn't see straight. Just the memory of her fingers tracing the muscles of his chest made him hard all over again. It was ridiculous.

He could hear the water of Sabrina's shower going in the next room and the vision of water running in rivulets down her silky skin, made him dash for the shower and turn the cold water on full blast. He shouldn't be thinking of her in this way. He had work to do, and he needed a clear head. He shuddered to think what was going to happen when they met up again. She must be so angry right now. There was no way that the drive to Sappho Farms was going to be anything but excruciating torture.

Sabrina was conspicuously silent when they met down in the lobby of the hotel. They walked to a coffee shop a block away, and Giles let her go ahead of him to order. When they got back to one of the small tables in the corner, they wedged themselves in between other early morning cafe patrons. Sabrina silently sipped her coffee and nibbled her croissant, avoiding eye contact at all costs. Giles opened his mouth a couple of times, but then closed it again. Sabrina was obviously still mad enough to kill him, but he had to smooth things over. He'd made it a practice over the years to avoid feminine tantrums at all costs, even if it meant saying he was sorry when he wasn't. It was the only way to manage a woman like Helene. Only this time it wasn't Helene and he was sorry, so he might as well get it over with.

"Look Sabrina, I don't know what came over me last night, but I am very very sorry. You have every right to expect me to give you the respect you deserve as a valued colleague."

Sabrina finally looked at him. He couldn't read her expression. "I think it would be a good idea if we pretended that last night, all of last night, never happened," she said.

Giles smiled with relief. "I would like nothing better. Please consider it gone."

"I will." Sabrina took another sip of coffee, the warm liquid settling her stomach. She wasn't sure she was going to be able to maintain her cool, but she had done a good job, all things considered. Giles must not know how little she resented his unwanted advances. In fact, she needed to maintain the fiction for her own sanity as well. Any more of Giles getting up close and personal and she would probably do something she'd regret. Probably a lot of things and a lot of regrets.

They finished their coffees and then walked back to the hotel, reclaimed their suitcases from the bellhop, and waited for the rental car to be brought around.

"A good day for traveling," Giles said.

Sabrina nodded. "I hope we can get some good ideas from Sappho Farms."

They maintained desultory conversation as they made their way slowly out of the city. But once they hit the less restricted roads beyond, they lapsed back into their former conversational rhythm. Giles asked a number of questions about Sabrina's childhood, and she found herself talking about her siblings, in particular the annoying but strangely endearing, Dave.

"What music does his band play?" Giles said.

"Bad heavy metal covers and some original stuff that is equally bad."

Giles chuckled. "Does Dave write the equally bad original music?"

"Yes. So, when he comes to visit I'm usually forced to listen to some new creation. This always leads to complaints from my downstairs neighbors. I can't say that I blame them."

"I would like to hear the band. Do they have a CD or something on iTunes?"

"You want to suffer permanent hearing loss?" Sabrina said.

"No, but I had a band back in the day, so maybe I'm feeling nostalgic."

"You were in a band?" Somehow she couldn't picture the suave Giles in rocker mode.

"In college, here in the U.S. That was one of my dreams – to be a rock star. That and be a professional cyclist, but I told you about that before. I was too tall to be really competitive."

Sabrina had a sudden vision of Giles in those super tight bike shorts and forcibly banished it. "What sort of music?"

"I wanted to be the next David Bowie. The 80's Bowie. The band was called Glass Knife. We thought the name sounded ironic."

Sabrina laughed. "Did you record anything?"

Giles shook his head. "We weren't that good. We played local gigs mostly. Then the other members decided to do more practical things like study for jobs in finance. Glass Knife withered to nothing."

"Do you still keep in contact with your bandmates?"

"As much as I can. We are all so busy, and when I was based in Europe, it was really hard."

Sabrina digested this. Maybe Giles obvious obsession with Helene was really due to a lack of company, female or otherwise, since he moved to Chicago. That might explain his need to drag Sabrina along on this farm odyssey. She was sure Giles' smooth demeanor and charismatic presence would win over anyone, even if they came from different worlds. Loneliness was a definite possibility. From what Sabrina could tell, Giles certainly didn't have many friends at work. The people who worked for him were universally afraid of him. Not because he had done anything nasty, but because he had curtailed the short days and long lunch hours that had been the norm in the department. Even the known suck-ups, who might have tried to work their way into his good graces, had been quelled by one intense look.

"I have a similar situation. All of my friends from before are somewhere else. Becky is my one true friend in the city."

"And now you have Oliver, of course."

"Yes, Oliver." Sabrina successfully directed Giles attention to a billboard and any further prying was averted.

When they finally pulled onto the drive that led to Sappho Farms, Sabrina had calmed her nerves. She finally felt ready to represent Federal Farm Machinery in a professional manner. The drive wound around for at least half a mile before Sabrina could see anything but trees and fields. And then around the bend she spied it – a long low building that looked suspiciously like a typical farmhouse that had been added on to over the generations. As they got closer, Sabrina made out a large painted sign over the covered front porch. It read *Sappho Farms* in large black script.

Three small children, one boy and two girls, stared at them from behind the railing of the porch. The children were four or five years old at best and dressed in dusty clothes that looked like they had seen several owners. Sabrina got out of the car and waved to them. This was not the welcome party she was expecting. She looked over at Giles, who seemed equally perplexed.

"Hello." Sabrina approached the porch. "We're the people from Federal Farm Machinery. Are Amy or Marci Hammer-Smith at home?"

The little boy piped up, "You mean Mom and Mama?"

"Yes."

The boy squinted at her and then pointed at the door of the house. "They're in there. Why are you here?"

"We just want to ask a few questions. Can we knock on the door?"

He shrugged his shoulders and Sabrina walked up the steps of the porch. Giles followed close behind her. She looked for a doorbell, but not finding one, knocked loudly several times. The door swung open and a tall woman with curly bright red hair done up off her face with a blue bandana, overalls and bare feet said, "Can I help you?" She had a small girl with a tuft of hair at the top of her head on her hip. The child took one look at Giles and Sabrina and wailed at the top of her lungs.

Giles stepped back instinctively, but Sabrina, who had spent many a Saturday night babysitting a set of twins down the street, smiled and said, "We must look pretty scary. We're the people from Federal Farm Machinery. I'm Sabrina and this is Giles. Can we come in?"

The redhead replied, "That's right, come in. Don't mind Bethany here, she cries at just about anything. Isn't that true love?" She leaned down and planted a kiss on Bethany's head. Bethany looked startled and stopped crying.

156

She stuck her thumb in her mouth, but her eyes continued to watch Sabrina and Giles suspiciously. "I'm Marci, by the way." The woman stuck her hand out and Sabrina gripped it.

"Thank you so much for letting us come talk with you. We are working on Federal's newest ad campaign, and as one of our best customers, we would love to get your input on why you have continued to buy Federal machines."

Marci shook Giles' hand and then said, "So you are getting tired of the hunks on tractors theme, huh?"

Giles smiled reluctantly. "Yes, we are."

"Too bad," Marci replied. "I kind of liked them. Not that they ever did anything for me, mind you, but they were pretty. I'm sure most of them were gay anyway, so I guess it doesn't matter if I wasn't their type and they weren't

157

mine. Has Federal ever thought about putting out a calendar? The *Men of Federal* has a sort of ring to it."

Sabrina laughed. "No, but if we can't think of a better marketing idea, we might have to do that or maybe franchise it as a Chippendales-type review."

Marci grinned. "See, I've solved your problem already."

They had just made their way past a cluttered family room with toys strewn across the floor like detritus on a shoreline into a spacious kitchen with a table that could have sat twenty people in a pinch, when a woman with curly dark hair entered from a door on the other side. She was dressed in a navy pant suit, with heels and a silk blouse.

"Hey Amy," Marci said. "These are the folks from Federal Farm Machinery."

"Hello." Amy shook hands with Giles and Sabrina. "Sorry, but I'm going to have to run again. I've got a meeting with some restaurant clients. Hey Marci, can you check on Kwame? I left him dealing with that pasture fence because I had to come back and change, but I'm not too confident about his skill set, if you know what I mean."

Marci nodded. "Sure. I'll take Sabrina and Giles around and we'll get over by the south pasture."

"Love ya babe." Amy gave Marci a quick peck on the mouth and then walked out of the room with a forceful step.

When she was gone, Marci said, "I was going to offer you a seat, but you don't mind walking a bit do you? Kwame just came to us a couple of months ago and he hasn't gotten the hang of farm chores yet."

"Of course. You have quite a family," Giles said.

"Yes we do. Amy and I just love kids, so we decided to foster some and one thing led to another. Now we have six adopted kids – four boys and two girls, and another six or seven we foster at any given time. Kwame's a sweet kid but he's had a rough time of it." She set Bethany down on the ground and looked around her. I know I left my boots somewhere."

The little boy from outside bounded into the room. "I'm hungry," he said.

"You know lunch isn't for another hour, but if you can find my boots, I'll let you have an apple." Marci grabbed one from the mound in a bowl on the kitchen counter.

"Ooh, I know." He ran out of the room and then came back carrying a pair of muddy rain boots.

"Good job Ben!" She gave him a high five and then the apple. He proceeded to eat noisily.

Marci led the way back outside, a trail of children in her wake. Those that had been hanging around the porch joined the procession.

Giles, who had never really had much experience with children, stuck close to Marci. Sabrina seemed much more at ease and, as they walked, she slipped farther behind, chatting with the children.

"I suppose we ought to get to the formal questions," Giles said.

"Fire away," Marci replied. She looked back at the children. "Sabrina seems like such a nice girl. You should hang on to her."

"We are just colleagues," Giles replied. "But she is very nice."

"Too bad. You know, I am rarely wrong about that sort of thing. I can usually tell a couple a mile away. That's how it was with Amy and me. I saw her at a party, with her arm around the shoulder of this girl she was dating at the time, and somehow I just knew. She was *the one*, you know what I mean?"

"Yes, I do." One look at Helene and Giles had fallen so hard his heart had broken in two.

Marci smiled. "Then I was right."

"No, no. Not Sabrina, someone else." Someone who was right this very minute preparing to marry another man. Giles felt his chest constrict.

"Yes, of course." Marci didn't sound convinced. "Anyway, what did you want to ask me?"

Giles' mind went blank for a moment as he replayed that final night with Helene in his head. He could almost feel smooth expanse of her skin under his hands, the lush contours of her full lips, the ecstasy of that last blissful moment before she had hurriedly thrown on her clothes and left his apartment. And before she had stopped returning his calls or texting him – ghosting him into this new lonely life in Chicago.

"Um." Giles pulled his head back into the present. "Basically we want to know what it is about our machines that bring you back as a customer?"

"Oh, that's easy. It's my dad," Marci replied.

"Your dad?"

"I inherited most of the land of Sappho Farms from him and he always bought Federals. I asked him once why he didn't buy something else. He told me that once you put your trust in a company and the company puts its trust in you, you stick together."

Giles nodded. "You don't usually see that kind of loyalty. Everyone is always chasing after the next big thing."

"I wouldn't stick with Federal if it were just my father's recommendation. We run a business after all," Marci said.

"Then why do you continue to buy our products?"

"The machines do what they are advertised to do. They are reliable and Federals are the only brand that can still be fixed by someone who isn't a computer technician."

"Really?" Giles said.

She nodded. "You wouldn't believe some of the stories we hear from the other co-ops. People go into farming because they love working the land and growing amazing food. They don't want to spend all their time rebooting the main console of a tractor."

Sabrina tagged along behind, engaged in conversation with a boy named Milton who at eleven knew the business of the farm backwards and forwards. He proudly informed Sabrina that he was in charge of milking the five cows they maintained in order to supply the house with fresh milk. The extra milk was combined with milk from a herd maintained on another piece for the co-op and made into artisanal cheese.

"That seems like a big job," Sabrina replied. "How long does it take you?"

"It's not how long it takes me – Mom says I'm the fastest milker she's ever seen – it's how early I have to get up to do it," he said proudly.

"And how early is that?"

"I have to be dressed and ready to go by four o'clock. Some days it's not even light out enough to see your hand in front of your face."

"Wow," Sabrina said, duly impressed.

Ben piped up behind them, "And he wakes everyone up with him, too!"

Sabrina turned back. "Brothers are supposed to annoy you. It is part of the job description. I have one, so I know."

Ben giggled and that sent the pack of them off in a bout of contagious laughter.

Sabrina smiled and said, "And what are all of your jobs on the farm?"

Each kid happily piped up. It was apparent to Sabrina that the kids all felt proud of the chores they performed, and that Marci and Amy had made a whole group of strange kids feel like one united family.

They finally reached the south pasture and came upon a tall lanky teenager. He had a mop of hair that probably spread out like a halo around his head if he hadn't had it restrained by a blue bandana. He was dressed in faded blue jeans and a dirty tee shirt with a pair of work gloves and some work boots, and stood defiantly with a hammer in one hand and a pair of pliers in the other.

"How's it going?" Marci said.

"I still can't get the gate to close. The metal's warped," Kwame replied.

"Hmm." Marci studied the gate. "Hey, Kwame, while I'm looking at this, these folks are from Federal Farm

Machinery. They are tagging along trying to get a handle on why we buy Federal machinery. You drive the tractors. Why do you like them?"

Kwame studied Sabrina and Giles carefully and then shrugged his shoulders. "I don't know. They run and they don't break down much. I can drive them pretty easy." He shrugged his shoulders again and relapsed into silence.

Marci crouched down and examined the hinges. Giles crouched down beside her, trying to look like he knew what he was doing. Kwame gave Marci the tools and Marci and Giles started to converse about the mechanics of the fence gate.

Sabrina pulled Kwame aside and said, "How long have you been driving tractors?"

"Since I got here."

"And when was that?"

"Two years ago." Kwame stared at a point beyond Sabrina's head, clearly tired of the conversation already.

"So what do you like best about living on the farm?" Sabrina said.

"The food's good. And it's quiet. You don't hear all sorts of cars honking and stuff."

"What's it like suddenly having such a big family?"

"Cool."

"Your little brothers and sisters bother you much?" Sabrina said.

"No, they're cool. Aren't you supposed to ask me about tractors?"

"Yes, but that is kind of a boring subject. I would rather find out about you."

Kwame looked at her directly for the first time. "Why?"

"I don't know. I'm not real close to my family, so I am curious about yours. You guys seem tight."

"Yeah."

Marci looked up and called over to them. "Are you filling Sabrina in on the farm equipment?"

Kwame nodded.

Sabrina said, "So I suppose I should get on with it. If you were to describe what it feels like to drive a tractor, what would you say?"

"Good."

Sabrina smiled. "How about a more descriptive answer?"

Kwame dug his toe into the dirt. "Look Lady. I don't know what to say. It's a tractor. It runs and it gets the job done. The important thing is the farm. The farm is the family and the family is the farm. That's what's important."

Marci finished tinkering and pulled the gate back into place. Giles stood up as well and straightened his tie.

Sabrina had to admit that he still looked amazing, even slightly rumpled and a little dusty. Damn him.

Marci corralled the little kids who had taken to running off in all directions and then the group meandered back to the house. When they reached the porch Marci said, "You folks are welcome to stay to dinner if you want. We usually serve it about two o'clock. Nothing fancy, mind you, but you can't get any fresher."

Giles declined on the grounds of putting them out, but Marci insisted that two more wouldn't make a difference and then promptly put both Giles and Sabrina to work cutting vegetables for a chopped salad.

The meal was loud and boisterous and amazingly delicious. It was something past five when they got back on the road. They were silent in the car as they wended their way to the airport and their late evening flight. Sabrina felt exhausted and might have fallen asleep if she were with anyone but Giles. There was something about the closeness of the car that made every muscle in her body tense up in expectation. It was electric, but also irritating. She just wished she could relax and go to bed.

"Did you get anything useful?" she finally said just because somebody had to say something.

"Not terribly much, but it was good to get away from the office." It was also a relief to finally have a topic of conversation. Giles had been racking his brain to hit upon something, anything, to say.

Sabrina sighed. "I was amazed at the way they handled all the kids. There was so much love there and so much gentleness."

Giles looked over at her quickly and back to the road. "I think you are just a little bit jealous."

Sabrina answered quickly. "I am not!"

He smiled at her reaction. "Well, I am. My mother was a good woman, but not patient. At least, not with me."

"She is no longer alive?"

"She died two years ago in a car accident. We were not close."

"I'm sorry. And your father?"

"He is alive and still in Belgium. I visit as often as I can. And your parents are?"

"Both alive."

Giles gave her another furtive look. Even in the dark of the car, he could sense her unease. He supposed grilling her about her family was completely inappropriate. Then again, he had done so many inappropriate things, that asking about family seemed a minor issue. He wasn't even sure why he cared to know about her family. But he did. For some unknown reason, he wanted to know more about Sabrina. "And are you close?"

"Not like Marci and Amy with their kids. I was closer to my grandmother than I am to my mom."

"Me too. I think grandmothers have a special, I don't know what. They just seem to understand."

"Yes." Sabrina smiled, recalling childhood memories. She felt some of the tension ease from her shoulders. "My Grandma Pearl was the only person who really connected with me. I was actually her favorite, I think."

"You are not your parents' favorite?" Giles said with a hint of mischief.

"Dave and I are definitely not the favorites," Sabrina replied with a wry laugh.

"Who is?"

Afterwards, Sabrina was never quite sure what possessed her to describe in intimate detail the precise relationship she had with her perfect sister, Tiffany. She also didn't ask why Giles, of all people, would be interested in her sibling rivalry. But he was, or so it seemed on their drive to the airport. Before she knew what had happened, they were pulling into the rental car return.

"Sorry to bore you," she said sheepishly.

"You didn't bore me. I am an only child, and so I have no interesting stories." He watched her expressive face as she registered disbelief and then laughed. "It is true, I promise you."

They made their way to through the terminal and then to the gate. Giles watched her call her apartment and speak with someone, presumably the boyfriend. Giles didn't have anyone waiting for him anywhere and so didn't bother to even extract his phone.

He wondered idly what Sabrina's boyfriend looked like – probably an ordinary looking guy. Nice. People tended to date people roughly as attractive as they were. Not that Sabrina wasn't attractive, but she wasn't Helene. Then again, there was something about her that had made him want to – he had taken a cold shower after all.

It was just loneliness, he decided. The break-up with Helene had hit him so hard he couldn't see his way straight on anything. Besides, men could be attracted to anything if given enough time alone. Even nice, normal girls like Sabrina. It suddenly dawned on him that Helene probably felt the same way about him. He was no Guy Lord.

Sabrina watched Giles out of the corner of her eye as she listened to Oliver's description of a documentary about the Franco-Prussian War he had found on YouTube. Oliver was trying to walk his way forward in history and had only gone that far. It was hard to assimilate everything that had happened in the world. But as she listened with half an ear, Giles continued to study her, his expression somewhere between interest and indifference.

Sabrina couldn't help but study him back. Even rumpled after a long day traipsing around the farm, he still looked better than most of the men she knew. There was something about the faintly Gallic shrug of his shoulders and the way his tousled hair naturally framed his face. He didn't seem quite as perfect as she had once thought. There was the lopsided way he smiled and the fact that one eye crinkled up more than the other when he spoke. And he had a habit of pausing too long sometimes before he spoke as if gathering his thoughts in English. But those quirks merely made her like him more. She realized suddenly that besides lusting after him, she actually liked him as a person. In fact, he had been really good company on this trip.

Oliver finally ran out of steam, and Sabrina was forced to give off looking at Giles and pay attention to her phone. "That is wonderful, Oliver. I think you've made great progress so far, but it is getting late. You really ought to try and sleep. I will be home soon, I promise. Uh huh. Yes. A kiss from me to you too. See you soon."

She hung up and turned her attention back to Giles.

"Everything okay at home?" he said.

"Yes, fine. Oliver was just telling me about a documentary he was watching."

"He is a student of history you said?"

She nodded, feeling suddenly very happy that she could claim to have a boyfriend, even if he was a strange man transported from some other Regency dimension into her life.

"What sort of history does he study?" Giles said.

Sabrina had actually thought up a backstory by this point and was happy to be able to trot it out. "He is pursuing a doctorate in British History – the Hanoverians, George III and the Regency and all that." Oliver had to be the foremost expert on that subject. "He is working on his dissertation now and so had time for a long visit."

177

"You must be very happy to have him here with you." Giles smiled at her with just a hint of wistfulness.

She felt her heart speed up. Could it be that Giles was actually jealous that she had someone and he did not? Just the thought made her want him more than she could say. She felt her cheeks flush crimson.

"Yeah," she managed after too long a pause. "Um, I think they just started calling our flight."

They were indeed calling the flight. Sabrina looked at her ticket and realized that she was actually in the first group. That was odd, but she figured someone had screwed up somewhere. However, when she got on the plane, she understood why they had boarded ahead of the masses.

"How are we in first class?" she said to Giles.

He shrugged. "I had them upgrade us. I figured it would be good to relax on the way home. There isn't enough room in coach."

"Oh," Sabrina said, trying very hard to look as if she weren't giddy with excitement. First class!

She stowed her bag and sat down in the window seat, which was distinctly more comfortable that her previous one in coach. Giles sat beside her and then stretched out. Their legs almost touched and Sabrina shifted her body towards the window. She could smell his cologne – the same dark musky affair that had a distinct European edge to it and her head spun with crazy desires.

"Comfortable?" Giles said.

"Oh, yes." She pushed her glasses up her nose with a suddenly sweaty finger.

A stewardess appeared and asked if they had any drink orders. Giles turned to Sabrina, "Would you like a glass of wine? It will not be great wine, but I think we deserve something for a good day of work."

Sabrina nodded. Wine did seem just the thing after the full day they had had. The wine came, a red for him and a white for her.

After remarking that it wasn't as close to vinegar as he had feared, they settled into a cheerful discussion of what, if anything, they could use from the visit for their marketing campaign. Two more glasses of wine followed, and Sabrina was having trouble keeping her eyes open. At some point she gave up and only startled awake with the rumble of the plane's tires hitting the runway, her mind a confused jumble of wine-soaked images. She opened her eyes and realized that she was no longer leaning against the plastic of the window, but rather the softer contours of Giles' Burberry sport coat. She sat up quickly, wiping her mouth, hoping against hope that she hadn't drooled on the expensive fabric.

He stirred at her movement, and she watched his beautiful face relapse back into angelic repose, fascinated at

180

the smooth contours of his cheekbones and the full lips,
parted just enough to show the edges of perfect white teeth.
She felt a longing sweep over her, more powerful than
anything she had ever felt before. She wanted him so badly
that it was like a physical pain settling down deep in her
bones. This perfect specimen of manhood, who would
never in a million billion years ever want her back, was the
one person she craved. She would have laughed at the
absurdity of the situation if she hadn't had brief glimpses of
the promised land – the kiss at the table and the midnight
knock at the door – that hinted that Giles in some alternate
universe might want her back. However, despite the
absurdity of Oliver's presence, this was definitely not an
alternate universe. She had to swallow her longing and
move on.

Sabrina hesitated to break the spell, but the plane
was skidding to a stop underneath them. "Giles," she

whispered. And when he didn't respond, she lightly touched his shoulder. "Giles. We've landed."

His eyes fluttered open and stared unfocused at her for a moment, his lips curling into a smile that trapped her with its warmth. "Sabrina," he replied.

"The plane has landed," she said.

He sat up slowly, his eyes still fixed on hers. "Thank you."

They stared at each other for a moment as if unwilling to end the sleepy idyll of the plane. The plane came to a definitive stop and the passengers around them stood to recover their luggage from the overhead bins. Giles stood and retrieved both of their bags. Sabrina realized that they were truly back to earth. She snapped back into the brisk demeanor she used at work.

She got out her telephone, turned off airplane mode, and then looked to see if she had any messages. She had several from Oliver, who had now clearly embraced the functionality of the telephone. He had reached World War I in his research and the brutality of the conflict had clearly gotten to him. Sabrina couldn't be sure, but she thought his voice sounded like he had been crying. She started to walk through what she would say to explain how humans had resorted to chemical weapons to resolve disputes over small amounts of territory and what she would say about the humans who went to war again thirty years later.

"You seem lost in thought," Giles said, breaking her out of her reverie.

"Just listening to Oliver's messages." She tucked the phone back in her purse.

"Of course." Giles stood to let her exit the plane ahead of him and they walked in silence through the bridge and back into the airport. When they arrived, Sabrina dug out her phone again to call a car, but Giles cut in. "My car is here. Let me drive you home."

As Sabrina wasn't about to look askance at the offer of a free ride, she quickly agreed. Giles kept up a light flow of conversation, mostly about terrible flight experiences he'd had, and Sabrina relaxed, glad that they had moved into the friendly banter zone. They walked to the parking garage and then to Giles' BMW. Of course he would drive a BMW.

Sabrina slid into the low-slung leather passenger seat, feeling very not like a Junior Copywriter living in a crappy apartment, eating Ramen more nights than she could count. She suddenly understood why young beautiful women married old rich men. This kind of luxury was intoxicating.

"Thank you for coming along with me," Giles said as he maneuvered around the garage to the exit.

"Of course. What is our next step? I will admit that I don't have any immediate ideas for the ad campaign."

"Me either at the moment, but I think we should run through all of our notes tomorrow morning and start brainstorming. There has to be something in what they told us that we can use."

Sabrina nodded.

"Now, where do you live?"

Chapter 9

Sabrina lived in a building that had certainly seen better days and in a part of Chicago that would charitably be called *up and coming*. Despite the fact that Sabrina told him to just pull up and drop her off, Giles circled the block looking for a place to park. His protective instincts refused to just leave her on the sidewalk. Besides, he was curious about her. She seemed fragile and yet tough at the same time. He wondered what it would be like to live in this part of the city as a single woman, alone. Then again, she had Oliver with her now. Giles wondered about him. Why wouldn't he have come to pick her up at the airport? Then again, maybe Sabrina had told him not to bother. That would be like her to not want a fuss made.

Once Giles found a spot down the street, he got out to open her door, but she, apparently unused to gentlemen opening doors for her, was already out with her bag slung over her shoulder when he came around the car.

"Thanks for the ride," she said.

"Let me walk you to your door," he replied. "And can I carry your bag?"

"Nope," she said with a laugh. "I've got it. And you don't need to follow me. I'm sure you want to get home too."

As he didn't really have any reason to get home, but wasn't going to admit that to her, he said, "I insist."

She shrugged her shoulders and took a step in the direction of her place. He followed a step or two behind. When they reached the door of the building, she pressed the intercom buzzer.

"Hello?" a male voice responded.

"Oliver, this is Sabrina. I'm coming up."

"My love," Oliver said. "I have so much to tell you."

Sabrina turned to Giles. "See you tomorrow."

"Thank you again for coming with me." Giles paused, suddenly uncomfortable. "I am sorry about everything – I promise it won't happen again."

She nodded, stepped into the vestibule, and closed the door behind her.

Giles turned as if to go and then looked up. There was a face in one of the windows above him but he couldn't make out the features. He waved and the face quickly disappeared.

Giles returned home in a funk. It was as if he were a balloon that had suddenly popped. He mechanically went through the chore of unpacking his bag and setting aside the clothes he needed to have picked up for dry cleaning. Then he worked out and took a shower. He played the events of the New York visit over and over again in his mind: seeing Helene again; kissing Sabrina; the strange dream that had taken him to the door of Sabrina's room; and the visit to the farm, where he'd seen a real family. He wondered what it must be like to have a real family here in Chicago. If Helene had stayed with him, he assumed that they eventually must have married and had children. Although now that he thought of it, he couldn't really see Helene as the maternal type.

Instead, it was the image of Sabrina that sprung to mind. Sabrina, who had seemed so at ease with the kids at Sappho Farms. Sabrina, whose rounded curves seemed more accommodating to the idea of a family. Not that Sabrina's curves were motherly – far from it – it was just that Giles could imagine things. He let his mind go off to that night in the hotel – the feel of her warm skin and soft body next to his. She would be all porcelain curves instead of hard angles. Thank goodness he had had the presence of mind to pull back. But now, in the privacy of his lonely apartment, he had to admit that he had wanted her in that strange moment of delirium. He had wanted her more than anything in the world.

Unfortunately, she was his subordinate and he had to keep things professional as best he could. Marilyn would literally have his head on a platter if she caught one whiff of anything she could use against him. Giles went to bed, fully intending to put any lewd thoughts of Sabrina out of his mind.

Sabrina, for her part, was having a harder time not wishing she had gone home with Giles. She had gotten through the very difficult explanation of Nazi genocide with Oliver, but he still remained somewhat shell-shocked. His horror was palpable, and Sabrina pushed the idea that he was an actor further away. Even a very good actor could not keep this Regency shtick up for days on end. She wrapped a blanket around Oliver's shoulders and held him close as if he were a small boy. "I know it is hard to understand, but we have moved past the horror, Oliver. That is why we still have so many documentary films about the war – so we can never forget."

"But women and children?"

"Yes dear. My grandmother's parents came to the U.S. to escape the Nazis in the 1930's."

"Your grandmother?"

"She is the one who gave me this necklace." Sabrina pointed to the locket around her throat. She had dug it out of her purse and put it on before they disembarked from the plane. If anything got snatched at night in Chicago, she didn't want it to be Grandma Pearl's necklace.

"Mrs. Dunhill?"

Sabrina chuckled, remembering that he still thought of her as Sabrina Dunhill from the book. "No,

Freiberg. Never mind. You can call her that. Her mother was Jewish and her father was Catholic. They left everything they had and came over here in 1935 because of the Nazis."

"You might never have been born?"

"I suppose not. However, she escaped, my mother was born and then I was born."

Oliver nodded. "Family is more valuable than gold." He sighed wistfully. "Why am I here, dearest Sabrina? Why have I been transported thus? I had thought it was to see the wonders of the future, but now I know that the future contains as much horror as wonder."

"I don't know, Oliver. I wish I did."

Later that night, as she lay next to a sleeping Oliver, her mind raced through all of the complications her normal boring life had acquired in the last several days. There was Oliver. There was Giles. And there was a marketing campaign that she had no idea what to do with. How was she ever to untangle any of this?

Her mind finally wound down enough to pass fitfully into slumber, but her dreams were confused and disorienting. She awoke to find early morning light streaming into her window and Oliver still asleep. She watched him a moment as she had watched Giles on the plane. He was equally angelically perfect, but the sight of his face just conjured up warm protective feelings, not the deep core of lust and desire she had experienced with Giles. Still, she supposed that one boyfriend was better than none.

She dressed quickly in the bathroom and then emerged to find Oliver standing at the counter of the kitchen, expertly working the coffee machine. He was dressed in a pair of gray sweatpants and a tee shirt that Sabrina had purchased from a clearance rack. Despite the cheapness of the garments, he was still undeniably attractive, and Sabrina had a moment of doubt. Who was she to push this man away, however strange his arrival in her life? He wanted her the way no one had ever wanted her. Perhaps, she should give in to those desires.

He turned and smiled at her. "I have become quite used to the coffee from this miraculous machine. It is very much superior to the coffee of my time, but not as good as the steam machine from that shop down the street."

Sabrina smiled in return. "At least the future has one advantage." She extracted the toaster from a shelf and plugged it in. Then she opened the bread and inserted two slices.

Oliver got out two plates, two knives and the jar of orange marmalade that Sabrina had splurged on. They ate their toast and drank their coffee standing at the counter in companionable silence. Sabrina reconsidered her celibacy once again. Oliver was easy to like and might be just as easy to love if she gave him the chance. So what if he seemed mildly deranged and might suddenly disappear as he had suddenly arrived? He was here now.

She was just about to take matters into her own hands and kiss him when she looked at her watch. Lord she was late for work! She set the plate and cup back on the counter with a clatter and ran back to the bedroom to retrieve her shoes and her bag.

"I'll be home as soon as I can tonight," she said as she ran for the door.

"Of course, my dear Sabrina. I will wait for you."

She was out of breath when she finally arrived at her cubicle and threw her bag on the floor. She looked over and noticed that Giles' office was dark. Where was he?

That question was answered soon enough when Giles came strolling in, carrying two coffees and what appeared to be a bag of doughnuts, and called out to Sabrina as he passed. "Miss March, my office in twenty."

Sabrina nodded. "Of course."

She heard the whispers from the other cubes but held her head up and stared at the computer screen in front of her. She was not about to let them rattle her. Besides, she had real work to do. The website text would not edit itself.

After nineteen minutes, she got up, grabbed a pad of paper and a good pen and then walked stiffly over to Giles office. She tapped on the door.

"Come in, Miss March," Giles said in a carrying voice as he opened the door. "I have some questions about the website." And when the door was firmly shut behind her, he added, "Now what are we going to do about this new marketing campaign?"

She sat down in one of the chairs in front of his desk, suddenly aware of the enclosed space of the office and the intoxicating smell of his cologne.

Giles sat down on the edge of the desk, entirely too close for Sabrina's comfort and grabbed one of the coffees. "Here, load up on caffeine. It might help."

Sabrina took the cup. "Thank you."

"Doughnuts?" He held out the bag.

"No, thank you. Maybe, later. I am afraid that I couldn't really come up with anything last night." In fact, she had been too busy explaining the Nazis to really put her mind to the sale of farm equipment.

Giles shook his head. "I didn't either. But let's think about what we learned. Why does Sappho Farms buy our products?"

"They are reliable."

"Right. Wait. He picked up the telephone and called his secretary, "Can you bring me one of those white boards with an easel?"

When the whiteboard was set up and the secretary had bustled out, Giles wrote *reliable*, on the board. "Okay, so what else?"

"You can fix the machines without having a degree in computers."

He nodded and wrote down *easy to fix*.

They went back and forth like this for over an hour, putting wards on the board, until all of the space was covered with Giles' spidery handwriting. By this point, Giles had taken off his jacket and loosened his tie, and Sabrina was pacing the floor, her cardigan discarded on a chair.

She paused and stared at the board. "There has got to be something in all of this. What is the one word that incorporates all of these concepts?" She absently reached up and touched the smooth metal of her locket. "Oh my goodness," she said with a start. "It has been staring us in the face all this time."

"What?" Giles said.

"Oliver told me that family is a treasure. And Kwame said the same thing. That is why they buy our tractors. It is nothing to do with the machines but what they help to preserve – family!"

"What do you mean?"

"I mean that the reliability and ease of use and all that is in the service of keeping the farm and all of the other farms in the cooperative going for the next generation. It is about the family!"

Giles stared at her for a moment and then a grin spread across his face. He reached out and pulled her to him in a ruthless hug. "My God, Sabrina you are amazing! Why didn't I think of that?"

Sabrina reveled in the feel of his arms around her. Too soon he would realize what he was doing and let her go.

He did after a minute and sheepishly disengaged. "I fear HR will have me impaled on a spike at this rate. Forgive me. But really Sabrina, you have exactly the right idea. We will design the campaign around family."

Sabrina certainly did not want to let him know how much she actually appreciated his totally inappropriate behavior, so she took a sip of coffee and replied, "It is just your Gallic enthusiasm that leads you into trouble."

Giles grinned. "It must be that. But we have no time to lose. Come, I will need your undivided attention until we can unveil this masterpiece at Farm Con."

When Sabrina finally got home, Oliver was already in bed asleep. Sabrina found the discarded Ramen package in the trash and sighed. Perhaps it was best. Thoughts of Giles seemed to crowd in upon themselves, and she was too tired for difficult conversations.

The weeks passed in a similar fashion – late nights and early mornings. Sabrina spent so much time with Giles that she should have been used to the sensual sound of his voice or the intoxicating smell of his expensive cologne, but every time he walked in the room, her heart seemed to do a little flip in her chest. And there were moments, sitting beside him in a meeting, when she could almost feel a wick of electricity pass between them. No, it had to be in her head. There was nothing between them but hard work.

Oliver seemed to take her prolonged absences in stride for the most part, but there was a tension around his eyes that worried Sabrina when she had a moment to contemplate his feelings in amongst the chaos of her work. He never once wavered in his position that he was the Earl of March and she was his new wife, and so Sabrina came to accept it, however crazy that might seem. Besides, Becky told her, based on years of watching Lifetime movies involving beautiful amnesiacs, that playing along might just help him come to his senses.

Giles had assembled a team consisting of the smartest people Federal Farm Machinery could muster, plus some really bright graphic designers and film folks Giles pulled in from the U.S. branch of the ad agency that had done the Legends campaign. This group specifically did not include Marilyn, who stalked around the office like a lion looking for its prey.

Sabrina was the most junior member of the group, but the others didn't seem to mind, particularly since Giles very freely gave her credit for the initial idea. It was amazing how much Sabrina could come out of her normally sarcastic shell once she wasn't viewed as a peon without a brain in her head. And the outside people, who hadn't known her before, seemed to take her new elevated position in stride. She was the happiest she had ever been at work, but she knew that once the new campaign launched, she was sure to be back under Marilyn's thumb as a Junior Copywriter once more.

Soon enough the day dawned when Sabrina loaded her rented car with two small suitcases and Oliver to take a road trip to Las Vegas. She would normally have flown out, but Oliver was showing signs of discontent and Becky had to visit family and so couldn't check up on him. He would certainly have enjoyed every minute of an airplane ride, but as a man without apparent identification, she couldn't exactly walk him through the TSA. She had explained the trip to Giles as the quintessential American vacation that an Englishman like Oliver had always dreamed of taking. Giles understood immediately – visions of Hollywood movies obviously dancing in his head.

The drive out of Chicago was uneventful enough, but once the car hit the suburbs, Sabrina learned the difference between car and buggy travel.

"Oh my Lord!" Oliver said as soon as the car hit forty miles an hour. He ducked down in the seat, covering his head. "How fast can you go in this contraption?"

Sabrina laughed. "At least eighty or ninety miles per hour. Don't worry, I can handle the car. If we don't go fast, we won't get there in three days."

Oliver unbent a little and looked at Sabrina. "How far away is this city of Las Vegas?"

"One thousand seven hundred miles. Roughly."

His eyes opened wide like saucers. "That is over twice the distance of England, end to end."

"The United States is a vast country. Look, I know that all of this is new, but you need to relax and let me handle the trip. It will be fine. And there is no place like Las Vegas in the whole world. I promise that you will love it."

He smiled timidly at her. "I am ever in awe of you, my beloved Sabrina."

Sabrina colored up. Oliver was so amazingly sweet. It hurt a little that she couldn't feel for him what she felt for Giles. "Thank you. Now sit up and enjoy the ride."

Once he got over his initial fear and some car sickness, Oliver settled in to enjoy the beauty of the American landscape. In fact, he was probably the best travel companion Sabrina could have asked for – enthusiastic, helpful and interested in every town they passed, every gas station they drove through and every motel they stopped in for the night. And, as Sabrina had predicted, when they finally arrived in Las Vegas at dusk, Oliver's mouth hung open.

"It is the most beautiful sight I ever beheld," he said when he could finally talk.

"I told you it was something amazing."

"It is beyond anything. What are these large buildings? They are all different shapes and sizes."

205

"Hotels and casinos," Sabrina replied.

"Casinos?"

"Places to gamble."

"As in Faro?" he said.

"Not Faro, but other modern games of chance."

"And which of these hotels are we to stay at?"

"The conference is in the Venetian. That is a hotel that looks like the city of Venice."

"Ah Venice! I went there on my Grand Tour."

"Then you can tell me whether it is anything like it. I have never been to Europe," Sabrina replied.

"Never been to the continent?" Oliver said.

Sabrina nodded.

Oliver sighed. "I would so love to show you the wonders of Italy. After Napoleon has been routed, of course. When do you think we will be able to go home again?"

Sabrina focused on the road. "I do not know. Someday."

Chapter 10

The hotel room was large and incredibly plush compared to her small apartment. And, as Sabrina was there for a work conference and would presumably be reimbursed, she felt free to eat at a rather expensive Italian restaurant in the Venetian complex.

She had just ordered a decent bottle of wine, when she heard a familiar voice calling her name. She felt the blood in her veins hum. She turned her head. "Giles?"

He approached the table. "Sorry to interrupt, but I'm glad you made it in to Las Vegas." He held out his hand to Oliver. "Hello, I am Giles, Giles Philippe. I work with Sabrina at Federal Farm Machinery. You must be Oliver."

Oliver had previously received a lecture from Sabrina about the new method of greeting via handshake, instead of bowing, and about the fact that no one in this casual future was going to call him by his title. He stuck out his hand and gripped Giles' forcefully.

Sabrina had mentioned Giles in a passing sort of way, as part of her colleague group, but was not sure how Oliver would take Giles obvious knowledge of Oliver's existence.

As it was, Oliver seemed to assume that Sabrina would of course have mentioned him to all her coworkers. "Giles, very pleased to make your acquaintance."

"And yours. Sabrina has told me so much about you."

Sabrina felt her stomach twist up in a knot. Oliver was bound to say something odd if allowed to converse with Giles for any length of time. She leaned into Oliver and gave Giles a look that she hoped would indicate her desire to spend time with her boyfriend in a romantic dinner for two.

Giles got her meaning. "Again, forgive my intrusion. I am on my way to my own dinner. Sabrina, we have a conference room reserved tomorrow morning to go through final preparations. I will text you the location. Eight o'clock sharp, okay?"

Sabrina sighed in relief. "Yes, of course."

Giles walked away from Sabrina's table, his mind in a whirl. He had never claimed to be a particularly good human being. He knew people were often beautiful on the inside and that body positivity was a thing everyone should strive for, but he admittedly judged books by their covers every day of the week. He had initially assessed Sabrina as a frumpy woman. That image had taken a turn when he kissed her and then again when he showed up at the door of her room, ready to make passionate love to her. Her subtle beauty had grown on him. Despite the shapeless shifts and the glasses that were still too big, he now found her strangely compelling.

However, Giles suddenly found himself at another abrupt bend in the road. He wasn't blind and he wasn't stupid. Sabrina's boyfriend Oliver would be considered an extremely attractive man in just about every context. In fact, he reminded Giles of a model they had used in one of the ads in the Legends campaign. And the way he looked at Sabrina – as if there was no one else in the room. Giles felt a stab of jealousy. How could he ever compete with that?

Giles stopped himself. Why would he be competing with Oliver? Since when had he seriously desired to date Sabrina? The answer hit him with the force of a ton of bricks. He had spent day after day in her presence, appreciating the quickness of her mind, and her smart sense of humor. He also admired the rounded curves of her body that emerged from the shapeless dresses as she casually brushed beside him. Then there was the smooth whiteness of her long elegant neck, the full pout of her lips, and the dark hair she casually pushed behind one ear. And she had the most beautiful eyes – large and crystal blue. Sabrina's beauty had worked its way into his subconscious until he could never quite free himself of her presence in his mind. No wonder a man like Oliver wanted her too.

It was a lie that he had dinner plans. In fact, he was as alone as he had always been since Helene's defection. He picked another restaurant in the complex and sat down at a table for one. It was near a secluded corner that housed the screened off VIP tables. He ordered an expensive bottle of wine with the plan of drinking the whole thing and then stumbling back to his room to sleep off his despair. The bottle came and Giles started in with gusto.

"Fancy meeting you here," a familiar voice said.

Giles looked up from his wineglass. "Helene?"

Helene St. Just stood in front of him – her exquisite face wreathed in an electric smile. Giles felt goosebumps wick up his arm. She wore a dress that seemed

212

more like a negligee but was certain to cost more than most women's entire wardrobe. Her long dark hair swished behind her as she cocked her head at him. "What are you doing here alone? Where is that girlfriend of yours?"

"I could say the same about Guy Lord," he replied.

Helene sat down, draping herself on the chair provocatively. "He is off in Vancouver shooting a film, and I am here all by myself on a photo shoot for Crave perfume. I am the new spokesperson in case you didn't know."

"I am afraid I have stopped following your career. You don't have an entourage to dine with?"

"No." Her eyes glittered with mischief, and Giles felt his stomach turn over with butterflies. "I gave my assistants the night off, so I am all by my lonesome. Why are you here, Giles?"

"I have a conference."

"Farm Con? How very American. I saw a banner in the lobby with a tractor on it," she said with a smirk.

He felt stung by her obvious contempt. "I know it isn't like a famous perfume or anything, but it is my work."

"You mistake me, Giles. I have nothing but respect for your work. But why you should waste your talents on farm equipment is beyond me. You had much better go back to Europe and pick up where you left off. In fact, I am sure I can get you in with the Crave team."

Although the thought of returning to his former life was excruciatingly tempting, Giles was not about to give Helene the upper hand. "Thanks, but no thanks."

The waiter appeared and seemed shocked that the famous Helene St. Just had not been properly seated in the VIP section. She laughed. "But I have just encountered my friend Giles. Come, Giles, sit and keep me company."

He considered turning her down, but the prospect of sitting with someone, even if it was the woman who had crushed his heart, was too great to resist. He got up with his glass of wine and followed her to a VIP table behind the screens. There were other VIPs already seated, but Giles didn't recognize any of them. A group at the next table seemed young enough and absorbed by their phones enough to be Instagram stars. They snapped selfies of the food and each other in between desultory conversation. They seemed to have recognized Helene, however, because Giles caught one of them surreptitiously snap a photo of their table. Helene didn't seem to notice. She stared absorbedly into her own phone.

After the meal came, Helene was in one of her more bubbly moods, and Giles, lulled into dropping his guard by the wine and the excellent dinner, began to drown in the melancholy that had caused his move to Chicago. Helene was the woman of his dreams, and he had irretrievably lost her. Sabrina had Oliver and he was alone. He would always be alone.

They had just finished the main meal, steak for him and a shrimp and vegetable sauté for her, when Helene's phone began to buzz on the table. She picked it up with a cross look. "I told them not to disturb," but she stopped, and her face went white. She punched in a number with one of her long acrylic nails. "What?" She almost screamed into the phone. "Wait. I'm at the restaurant. Come get me. They are going to be all over this." She pounded the phone with another talon and threw it down on the table.

"What is wrong?" Giles said.

Helene replied, "I am going to kill him!"

"Who?"

"Guy!" Helene looked at Giles as if not seeming to see him. Then she snapped back into focus. She smiled, beckoning him with her eyes. "You need to help me."

"Me?"

"Yes. You can explain later to that little girlfriend of yours." Helene turned to the next table. "Hello, I am Helene St. Just. Could you possibly do me a favor?"

The kids at the table agreed. A young woman, who seemed entirely too perfect to be real, said, "What do you need?"

"A good photo of me and my friend Giles." Helene handed her phone over. "None of my selfies have turned out."

"No problem. I suspect your settings are off." She fiddled with the phone and then put it up. "Now smile!" After several photos, Helene naturally offered to take some photos with them.

Giles watched Helene, surprised at her sudden change of emotion. He had never known her to act so friendly with strangers. And then another woman appeared, who Giles faintly remembered as one of Helene's assistants.

She carried a pair of sunglasses and a trench coat in a large

Louis Vuitton bag and proceeded to dress Helene.

"How many are there?" Helene said.

"I saw two coming in. I have gotten you a suite at

the Bellagio under the name of Elizabeth Hunter." She

regarded Giles suspiciously. "Is he coming?"

Helene turned to Giles and laid a hand on his arm.

"You'll help me, won't you? I just need you to walk with

me to the elevators. There may be some press looking to

follow me."

Giles agreed, sure that the more time he spent with

Helene the more his body would ache with withdrawal

when she inevitably left him, but unable to refuse her.

They made their way through the restaurant with

little fuss, but when they stepped out into the casino, a

small scrum of reporters pounced. Helene slipped her arm

through Giles' and walked forward; her face impassive

behind the sunglasses. Some man claiming to be from TMZ

stuck a microphone in front of Helene. "What do you have to say to Guy Lord right now?"

Helene pulled Giles closer. "No comment, thank you."

"You don't have anything to say?"

"No comment. Please let me go," Helene said.

"And who is this man with you?"

"An old friend. Now please let me go."

The conversation continued on like this until the little group made it to the elevator and forced the door to close.

"My God Helene, would you please tell me what on earth is going on? Why are all of these reporters tailing you?" Giles said.

Helene removed the sunglasses and made as if to dab her eyes. "There are photos of Guy in Vancouver with – with some slut in a nightclub. They are all over the

Internet." She gave Giles a look that he knew of old – the look that said she wanted something. Giles tensed. Helene could have easily bended him to her will in the past with one flutter of her eyelashes. He didn't know if he was strong enough to resist her now.

"Giles," her voice slid over him. "It is too much. I can't be alone right now. You must come with me to the Bellagio."

Giles felt his rational mind pulling forcefully against the suddenly very strong desires of his heart, and his body. "No Helene. I have work to do here. I can't just spend all night picking up the pieces of your love life."

"But Giles," she pouted. "I am all alone here, and I need a shoulder to cry on. You said we would always be friends."

Previously, this sort of plea would have caused Giles to cast aside whatever he was doing and run to Helene's side. But the desire to immolate himself on the pyre of her whims had faded. He studied her face. She was beautiful, but he could now see how she used her beauty to work on him. Did he really think she would ever come back to him? Did he really think she would ever look at him the way Oliver looked at Sabrina?

He replied, "You said we would always be friends, but that was only after you dumped me. Do you know how hard it was to get over you?"

"Fine," she replied bitterly. "But have the decency to walk me to my car. God knows how many reporters are going to be on the other side of that door."

He reluctantly agreed, resolved to hand her into the car and then return to his room to get some sleep before the conference. Unfortunately, the reporters seemed to have been following Helene with GPS. They opened the elevator to the blinding flashes of cameras. Helene grabbed his arm and pulled him forward with her into the dark interior of the waiting limousine.

He tumbled onto the seat, and Helene's assistant crowded in after him, pulling the car door closed. The engine roared and the limousine lurched forward. The young woman keeled over against him and he fell against Helene like a series of dominos. He righted himself as soon as he could.

"I thought I said I didn't want to go with you to the Bellagio," he said.

Helene ignored him while the assistant barked orders into her phone.

Giles sighed. Once they got to the Bellagio, he would plot his escape.

Sabrina and Oliver ate in a leisurely fashion and ordered another bottle of wine. Oliver could apparently drink wine by the gallon, and when Sabrina made light of it, Oliver looked at her with a furrowed brow.

"But of course, my dear. I have been drinking wine since before I was breeched. This water you have here is wondrously good, but it was not always so."

Sabrina nodded, aware yet again of the small blessings of her own time. Oliver had given her so much food for thought in the weeks he had been in her life. Oliver smiled at her. He had such a delightful smile. Sabrina felt her resistance against Oliver's charms melt away in the haze of the alcohol and the warmth of that smile. She didn't know why or how he had come into her world, and she had no way to predict how it would all end, but she realized as she sat in a fancy Italian restaurant across from a man who was her literally her fantasy, that she should give over worrying and just enjoy the ride.

They walked hand in hand to the elevator and Sabrina thought he might lean in to kiss her when the doors closed, but he was still very unsure of the mechanics of the elevator. He held her hand with white knuckles as he gripped the wall. Once they were on solid ground again, he gave her his arm like a proper gentleman until they were safely behind the closed doors of their room.

He leaned down and kissed her gently as if afraid to scare her, but this time she threw caution to the winds and kissed him back with all of the longing she had stored up as a lonely girl. She could feel how his body stiffened in surprise, but she continued the attack, pushing him farther into the room towards the king size bed. He recovered his equanimity enough to pull away and say, "My love, are you sure?"

"I am," she replied as she tugged at the collar of his shirt and tried to work the buttons free. Why did men's shirts have such small buttons?

He gently took her hands in his own. "Sabrina, darling, we must speak."

"What?" she replied. What was it about Regency men that they had to talk so much? Did they not want to have sex?

He pulled her to the bed and made her sit beside him. "Sabrina, my lovely wife."

"Girlfriend."

"Yes, well, whatever you say in this time. Dear, before we consummate our relationship, there are certain things you must know about when a man and a woman make love. I know that your mother has probably discussed aspects of the marital relationship, but I do not want an unwilling or a frightened bride. I will be gentle, but you have to know that it may hurt a little bit the first time. It will be better after that, I promise."

Sabrina stared at him, not totally comprehending. And then it hit her in a rush. Of course, he would expect her to be a virgin. "This is completely unnecessary. Sweet, but unnecessary. I hate to break it to you, but I am not a virgin. Very few women in their twenties are in this day and age. Things have changed."

His mouth dropped open for what seemed like ages and then he shut it. He swallowed hard. "You mean I am not the first man?"

"No. I had a fling in college. Although, I wouldn't really call him a man. He was pretty immature. Anyway, that's how it is now. Young women can have sex before marriage just like young men. You are not a virgin either, are you?"

He colored up. "No, but that is to be expected. Young men must have some outlet for their, er needs."

"And so do young women. Look at it this way, you will not find me frightened or unwilling. I enjoy sex, believe me, whenever I can get it."

"You mean that it is common in this time for men and women to make love when they are not married?"

"Yes. In fact, it is pretty uncommon not to, unless you have some religious objection."

"But how do they not have children out of wedlock?" Oliver's brow furrowed in confusion. "Or do they?"

"You can, of course. It is not the sin it once was. But there are ways, either with pills or condoms, or something else." She looked down, slightly embarrassed. "But I'm not on the pill, so we need to talk about protection."

He seemed dazed. "Protection?"

Sabrina got up and then dug through her suitcase for the box of condoms she had thrown in on the off chance something exciting happened to her. It was a little battered as she had had it floating around her apartment for a while, but still viable. She handed it to Oliver, who looked it over and then cautiously opened it up.

227

He studied one foil packet. "What am I to do with this, exactly?"

Sabrina figured sacrificing one couldn't hurt. She took the packet and ripped it open. "See, this is like a rubber sheath that goes over your, um, member."

His eyes brightened. "I have seen these before, but what a wonderful material. It cannot be sheep intestine?"

"No, it is latex. Were condoms back in the day really made of intestines?"

"Yes, with a string to tie them on. But this latex as you call it is so fine that it must often break. I am sure you cannot get more than a couple of uses out of it."

"You are only supposed to use it once!" Sabrina replied.

"Oh. I suppose that is more hygienic. But why must we employ such a device?"

"So I don't get pregnant, and we don't give each other some disease."

"You have a disease?" he said with a horrified expression.

This conversation had gone so far from the initial promising beginning that Sabrina's embarrassment turned to laughter. "No, I have been tested, thank you. You, on the other hand, I am not so sure."

"I do not have the pox!" he replied hotly.

Sabrina was really laughing now – so hard that tears formed at the back of her eyes. "Of course not! No Regency hero ever has a disease no matter how many women of easy virtue he has conquered. Isn't that how it is supposed to be? Isn't that the myth that every Regency novel sells?"

"What are you talking about?"

Sabrina realized she had hurt his feelings. "Sorry, my tongue got away from me. I am sure you don't have a disease, but a condom is still a good idea."

"Doesn't it alter the sensation terribly?"

Sabrina had to control a scoff. "I am sure that that thing made of intestines did do a lot of things, but a latex condom will not stop you from any necessary sensation."

Oliver nodded, but still looked pensive. "How are we to have children, then?"

"I think it is best we don't have any until we figure out this whole time problem."

He seemed on the point of arguing with her but then sighed. "I suppose you are right. Why is everything so complicated is this time of yours?"

"I don't know. It just is."

Oliver leaned over as if to kiss her, but then stopped. He got off the bed and went to his suitcase. He pulled out a dog-eared paperback. Sabrina realized it was *To Kiss an Earl*. He handed it to her. "You mentioned novels. I found this some time ago, but I wanted so much to be with you and enjoy this new world of the future, that I didn't dare ask you. What is this book?"

"It is the story of how you fell in love with Sabrina, the woman who became your wife, written by Paige Lindsey"

"You say that as if Sabrina wasn't you."

"I don't think I can be because I live here in this time and place."

"And this lady author, she writes as if she reads my very thoughts. In fact, she knows my thoughts and actions better than I do."

"So you have read it?"

He nodded. "In truth, there are parts that made me blush for my displays of vanity and pride."

Sabrina smiled. "Your pride is under good control."

Oliver gave Sabrina a soulful look. "By you I was properly humbled."

"Wrong book, but you clearly have understood the plot of *To Kiss an Earl*. However, I don't know that I am the Sabrina of the book."

"Then why am I here?"

Sabrina stood up and started to pace. "I don't know, Oliver. I don't know why you are here, except that my lonely desperation and psychotic fixation on *To Kiss an Earl* somehow magically called you up out of thin air."

"That is a very poor excuse for what must have a logical, rational explanation. This is an age of reason as much or more than my own. Surely there is some science there. Just as there is with the magical device you call a telephone in your reticule."

Sabrina looked at him. He was one hundred percent serious, but Sabrina couldn't come up with any science to explain it.

"I am sure you are right," she said. "There has to be an explanation."

He held out his hand to her. "And I am not confused about who you are. You are my lovely tempestuous Sabrina, with your beautiful eyes and your dark hair and porcelain skin. And your lips as sweet as honey."

Sabrina put her hand in his and let him pull her down beside him.

"I know that you are the only woman I could ever love."

Sabrina sighed. "You are very sweet Oliver, but I can't take advantage of your sweetness." She looked deep into his eyes. "I don't know how or what brought you here, but I am not the Sabrina of *To Kiss an Earl.* I wish with all my heart that I were. I wish I could go back in time and be the heroine of a great love story, but I am just an ordinary woman living an ordinary life."

"No. You are my Sabrina, and that is more than enough."

She sighed again, already half regretting what she was about to say. "I am not. The proof is that I don't love you – not the way Sabrina Dunhill does. And as I don't love you, I probably shouldn't sleep with you, no matter how sorely I am tempted. You deserve that Sabrina and that happy ending, not me."

Chapter 11

Giles was not in a good mood that morning. He should have known that extracting himself from Helene's grip would be a project. First, it had been the hysterical sobbing that had prevented him from leaving her. Second, Helene, sensing that he was on his way out the door, had turned on the charm, reminding him of all the reasons why he had fallen so hard for her. Finally, she planted a kiss on him, as they sat together on one of the couches in the suite. Ironically, the kiss had broken the spell. Helene leaned over and their lips met. Giles waited for the explosion of hormones that had made him such a slave to her, but the more she deepened the kiss, the more his mind seemed to rebel. Images of Sabrina as she stood in the door of her hotel room, the sensual curves of her body apparent under the thin fabric of an oversized tee shirt, flooded his brain.

Giles pulled back and stood up. "Don't do this to me Helene. You and I both know you are using me. And I am done with being used and then thrown away. If you are upset with Guy, then go deal with him."

She protested, but no amount of pleading moved him. He left the suite and felt an immense sense of relief as the door clicked behind him. His watch told him that it was three o'clock in the morning. However, it was impossible to sleep. He escaped the hotel and walked aimlessly down the strip, his mind a confusion of thoughts. He had to get a handle on his feelings. He had to stop his brain from constantly fixating on Sabrina. She was a work colleague. She was not his type. She was taken. And who was he to even think she would be interested? She was as good as dating a model, and the model was obviously absolutely crazy about her. What had Giles got that she would want?

A broken heart? A lonely apartment? A workaholic schedule that didn't leave room for anything else? Those things were hardly competition for a boyfriend like Oliver.

When Giles had wasted enough time, he returned to the Venetian and took a shower and changed into fresh clothes. He got himself a triple espresso and sipped the bitter coffee as he made his way down to the conference room. He felt edgy, nervous and incredibly cranky from the lack of sleep and the emotional residue of dealing with Helene.

There were already a couple of people milling about and Giles put them to work. The booth had been set up the night before, but there was a multimedia presentation to run through, with a large panel discussion about family farming featuring Marci from Sappho Farms. Giles sent someone to check and make sure Marci and Kwame were ready to go. Sabrina had specifically asked for

Kwame to attend as the originator of the new marketing slogan and one look at the Kwame's star struck face when he walked into the hotel, had reinforced Sabrina's good sense.

Sabrina showed up at a quarter to eight. She tried to project excitement, but Giles noticed a certain tension in her smile. He didn't have time to inquire further. There was too much to organize, too much to do. He made a mental note to circle back with her later. They dug into the work and then decamped to the large hotel conference room to set up for the panel.

Sabrina had also spent a long night. Oliver was still adamant that Sabrina was the woman from *To Kiss an Earl*. She had argued until she couldn't anymore and then fell asleep from sheer exhaustion. She awoke to find herself wrapped in Oliver's arms. There had been a moment in the seconds before her mind reached full consciousness that she thought of cuddling closer, but then she was awake and her brain switched on. She couldn't keep going like this. She dressed quickly, wrote Oliver a note so he wouldn't worry, and silently left the room.

Down with her colleagues, Sabrina switched into work mode and tried to forget about Oliver. Giles spoke to her briefly when she walked in the room, but then seemed to drift away. He appeared more than usually tense, and Sabrina thought about asking if he was okay, but got caught up. Once the panel was over, there would be more than enough time for conversation.

She was deep in a discussion with one of the ad agency guys when a woman from Federal sidled up to her. Holly was about a decade older than Sabrina, but still young enough to be addicted to her phone.

"Hey, did you see this?" Holly said.

Sabrina excused herself with the ad guy. "What?"

"Look at what TMZ just posted. Did you know Giles was dating a supermodel?"

Sabrina squinted at the phone, suddenly unable to breathe properly. The headline, "Helene St. Just Steps Out with a New Mystery Man," appeared under a photo of Helene and Giles, arm in arm. Sabrina's mind raced. It wouldn't do any good to admit that she had a clue about Giles' love life. "Wow," she replied with feigned surprise. "He never mentioned that to me!"

"Me either, obviously. To think we work with a quasi-celebrity. Where did he ever meet Helene St. Just, do you think?"

"Must have been the Legends campaign. She was in that," Sabrina said airily.

Despite her careless manner, Sabrina's heart pounded in her chest. Giles had reconciled with Helene! Sabrina supposed that it had to happen, but somehow she still felt like she had taken a blow to the gut. She pulled herself together. No matter what strange whim had impelled Giles to show up at her hotel room door in the middle of the night, there had never been anything to it. A man like Giles would never actually want an ordinary woman like Sabrina. She crushed the last flicker of hope out under the heel of reason and turned her full attention to Holly.

Holly nodded. "You're right. She was in Legends. Still, it's got to be a rebound thing. Guy Lord was caught hooking up with some chick at a club yesterday."

"I saw that too. But maybe they had both moved on at the same time? It is hard to keep up with celebrities."

Holly smiled. "It is. Who knew we'd be this close to one. Do you think anyone at the conference will say anything?"

Sabrina shook her head. "Until they put a name with Giles' face, no one is going to look for him at Farm

Con. I mean, when you are milling around this place, do you think you are going to meet anyone involved with a celebrity scandal?"

"Only the country music headliners they have for the opening keynote speeches."

"Exactly." Sabrina sounded confident, but inside her head she was running some calculations. TMZ wasn't known to sit on its scoops and she was pretty sure that Giles had not shown any particular agitation when he stopped by their table the night before. Although it was possible that Giles had always planned to meet Helene here beforehand, Sabrina figured that he would have seemed happier than he had been. In fact, given their fake kiss, Sabrina would have been the one person he would have told, right? So, that meant that he had encountered Helene afterwards and then been discovered by TMZ. And that meant that TMZ was probably still skulking around, trying to locate information. That could be bad.

She reminded herself that she didn't have time to worry about Giles. There were too many real details to keep her occupied. The whispers about Giles continued as the group migrated to the large conference hall to set up for the panel, but no one seemed willing to confront him while he was in the middle of his work. They set up the presentation, ran through some technical trials and then gathered the panelists and arranged them according to plan. Giles acted as the conductor – making sure that each part of the presentation hit the right note. Once the panel was done, the full marketing campaign would go live on the Internet, to be followed in due course by television, radio and print media.

The large conference room started to fill, first with early birds and then in earnest. Apparently there were a lot of people interested in hearing about family farming and Federal Farm Machinery. Sabrina took a seat down in front,

243

off to the side and Holly joined her. From their vantage, they could sit sideways and see the whole room. Marci arrived with Kwame and he took the spot next to Sabrina. He had been given Marci's phone to hold, but apparently had memorized her passcode, because he opened up a game and started to play.

"Boy, this is a lot of people," Holly said. "We certainly didn't have this kind of crowd last year."

Kwame looked up from Marci's phone. "Must be your boy, Giles."

"What?" Sabrina said.

"He's dating that supermodel. TMZ just put out his name. See." Kwame shoved the phone under Sabrina's nose. The story had been updated to include a blurb about Giles.

"Damn," Sabrina replied. "Oops. Kwame, sorry."

Kwame shrugged. "I've heard worse."

"My love, I have found you at last."

244

Sabrina shot out of her chair. "Oliver?"

Oliver made his way up the aisle towards her. "You left so quickly this morning and with such stealth that I became concerned. Some person told me that I could not enter this part of the hotel, but I was able to slip in when he wasn't looking. It is truly marvelous the number and variety of farm implements you have now. I would love to tour the conference further. What is this theater piece we are about to see?"

"It is not a play. They will be speaking about family farming. Come, sit down and you shall see."

Holly seemed a little surprised when Sabrina introduced Oliver as her boyfriend, but made room for him just the same. Kwame barely looked up from the phone.

"I have been wandering this hotel trying to find you. Did you know that they have a canal in miniature? It was the most wondrous reconstruction I have ever beheld.

245

The water is too blue and clear, however, to be real. Still, we must go when the play is done."

Sabrina was about to reply, but then Giles ran up the dais and grabbed the microphone. "Thank you all for coming today to hear from our esteemed panelists. We at Federal Farm Machinery know that family is the reason that you farm. This is why we are very pleased to present our new slogan, *Family. First.,* and to sponsor today's panel." Images from the ad campaign flashed up on the screen – the smiling children of Sappho Farms bathed in golden sunlight.

"Now let me introduce our very first brand ambassador, Ms. Marci Hammer-Smith, from Sappho Farms." Marci stood and there was a round of generous applause.

"Next to her is Mr. Frederick Banner, a renowned economist specializing in —" Giles paused and put his hand up to his eyes as if to see beyond the lights of the stage.

There was a commotion of some kind at the back of the room. Everyone swiveled around and craned their necks to see.

Flashes of light and clicks of machines indicated that a scrum of reporters had gathered. Out of the confusion emerged Helene St. Just, dressed in a tight white dress that made her look like a Roman goddess. How in the hell had she gotten into the conference area? Sabrina heard the quick intake of breath that rippled through the crowd as the identity of the woman in white registered in the startled brains of the Farm Con attendees.

"Wow," Kwame said. "How did Giles get a girl like that?"

Giles seemed frozen to the spot on the stage. Marci leaned into her microphone and coughed, and when that didn't snap Giles out of it, she said, "Miss St. Just, I am so glad you take an interest in family farming. Now sit down so that we can continue."

Helene, who was obviously not used to being ordered around, looked like she was about to spit fire. She didn't have the chance, however, because there was a shout from the other side of the room. "I am going to kill the bastard!"

If Helene St. Just commanded a turn of the head, whatever was going on on the other side of the room inspired row upon row of lanyard-wearing conference goers to stand up and head in that direction.

Helene screamed at the top of her lungs and stamped her foot, causing the conference lemmings to move back towards her.

Sabrina, shorter than just about everyone around her, stood up on her chair to see. "Oh my God. That's Guy Lord!"

"Where is he?" Guy shouted. He was surrounded by an entourage of dark-suited men, who seemed to be struggling to hold him back.

"Guy, don't even think about coming over here!" Helene shouted back. Her assistant and a couple of bodyguard types burst through the doors of the conference room. They approached Helene cautiously. Sabrina wondered if Helene often put them in the position of having to talk her down off of ledges.

Giles finally pulled himself together. He called out to Guy, "There is nothing between Helene and me."

"Like hell!" Guy replied. He wrestled with his people and then broke free, dashed across the conference room and up the dais steps.

Sabrina would later recall what happened next as if seeing it all in slow motion. In some misguided attempt to help, she hopped down from the chair and rushed up the dais steps to Giles' side. She arrived just in time to see Guy Lord pull back to take a swing at Giles. Giles tried to duck, but he wasn't quick enough and Guy's fist connected with Giles' temple. Giles' eyes rolled back and he crumpled down. Sabrina screamed and clutched at him, preventing him from hitting the ground at full velocity, but his dead weight pulled her with him and she landed on the ground on top of him. She scrambled back off and looked down into his face. He was as white as a ghost and not moving.

"Giles!" Sabrina cradled his head, tears streaming from her eyes. Her heart beat so fast she thought it would burst out of her chest. "Giles. Open your eyes. Giles, please don't die on me. Please. Please. Come back to me." His eyes fluttered open, seemed to focus on her face for a second, and then closed.

Paramedics eventually arrived with a stretcher and pulled Sabrina away. After they ascertained that she wasn't seriously injured, they hustled her off to the side. Then the police arrived to question everyone who was within sight of "the incident," as they were now calling it. Oliver wanted to hover protectively around her, but Sabrina, fearing that a man without identification who claimed to be an English earl under the reign of George III, would not be viewed favorably by the authorities, told him to wait for her outside the ballroom. He started to argue, but Sabrina would have none of it and he eventually left. Guy Lord and Helene St. Just were nowhere to be found and Sabrina imagined that security had hauled them off to undisclosed locations to complete their interviews with police.

When Sabrina was finally able to extract herself from police questioning, she went in search of Oliver. She felt completely and absolutely numb. She tried not to think about Giles because every time she did her heart raced so fast that she thought she was having a heart attack. Numb was a better alternative. She sent Giles a text thanking him for taking a chance on her at work and being a good friend. If, no, *when* he did recover, he would know that she cared. Part of her wished she could confess her love as well, but that would just make things unbearably complicated.

She found Oliver waiting for her and thanked her lucky stars that he was at least compliant. Holly stood next to him, apparently keeping him company. Sabrina hoped against hope that Oliver hadn't said something weird.

"I think I need a stiff drink," Holly said. "You guys want to join me?"

"Yes," Sabrina replied.

They decamped to a sports bar outside of the conference area and ordered cocktails. Oliver was immediately struck with the quality of his whiskey and soda. "This is the smoothest whiskey I have ever had the pleasure to drink," he said. "I must discover the process of distillation."

"I am sure the Johnnie Walker website will have all sorts of information." Sabrina pulled it up on her phone and handed it to Oliver. Then she turned to Holly. "Who is in charge now?"

"They are sending Marilyn in to take control of the project, which I am sure is going to just make things worse."

Sabrina groaned. Really, this day was not getting any better. "Marilyn hasn't been involved with any of the roll out, so how is she supposed to manage it now?"

Holly shrugged her shoulders. She fiddled with her phone. "Look, #FederalFarm is trending on Twitter."

"Oh lord. That is all we need. I bet someone has already put out cell phone footage of the whole thing."

Holly nodded. She held the phone out to Sabrina. "See, it is the lead story on TMZ."

Sabrina dejectedly took another sip of her Cosmopolitan. Then she looked up at a large television above her head. The channel had switched to a News Break and Marci and Kwame appeared with the reporter. "Holly, look up," Sabrina said.

The sound on the TV was turned low, but they could still make out the conversation.

"Yes, my son and I were in the room when Helene St. Just and Guy Lord appeared. I was on the panel ready to talk about family farming," Marci said.

"Guy Lord came out of nowhere and clocked Giles," Kwame added. "Giles hadn't done anything – he was just introducing my mom."

"So, the attack was unprovoked?" the reporter asked.

"Totally," Marci replied. "Look, I know that this is sensational news involving celebrities, but Giles Philippe and the whole Federal Farm Machine team are the victims here. They have great products and a great story to tell about the value of family farming and all of that was cut short by some hot-head actor. Shouldn't you be focused on that?"

The reporter looked at the camera with a barely disguised eye roll. "I am sure, but tell me, what did you think when you saw Helene St. Just and Guy Lord crash your panel?"

"I was hoping they were going to join us in promoting sustainable organic farming. I should have known that a pair like that wouldn't do anything so self-sacrificing."

The reporter ignored the sarcasm. "And can you tell us more about the man at the center of this scandal? Who is Giles Philippe?"

"He is the person behind the Federal Farm Machinery advertising team. Well, he and Sabrina March.

We have gotten to know them and the whole Federal team as part of our spokespeople roles. You couldn't ask for a nicer guy."

Sabrina blanched at the mention of her name. That was all she needed.

Holly chuckled. "Glad you got the credit and not me."

At that point another bar patron called out, "Can we actually get some sports in this place?"

The bartender grabbed the remote and flipped the channel. The rest of the bar clapped.

"So much for local news," Sabrina said.

Holly turned back to her phone. "Hey, now #GilesPhilippe is trending."

"Is there any word on his condition in the Twitterverse?" Sabrina asked anxiously.

"Not yet – people are just bringing up the whole Legends thing and the TMZ report that seems to have triggered Guy Lord."

Sabrina sighed and tried to push down a spurt of panic. If anything happened to Giles – she couldn't even finish the thought. They were nothing but work colleagues.

Sabrina finished her drink and dragged Oliver away when he had finished his second whiskey. She had to get up and move. She had to do anything that would distract her. They wandered down to the canal and aimlessly window shopped. Oliver carried on a light patter of conversation about the marvels of the artificial water scene. When that began to pall, he relapsed into commentary on the number and quality of the merchandise on offer.

Sabrina tried to pay attention, but her mind wandered dangerously. In fact, she didn't notice that Oliver had stopped speaking until he took her hand and said, "Sabrina, I must tell you what is in my heart."

"What?" She turned back towards him. "Sorry, I have been wool gathering. That is the correct term, right?"

He nodded. Sabrina noticed for the first time a crease between Oliver's brows. He seemed tired. Perhaps Las Vegas was too much of a leap from Regency England. She should lead him back to the hotel room to rest.

He took her other hand and held both hands in his. "My love, I must return home."

"Don't worry, we will likely be sent back to Chicago tomorrow now that all of this has happened with Giles," she replied.

"No. I mean my true home. In the time I was born and raised."

"But —"

"Please, Sabrina, I have loved every minute of this new and exciting world, but you cannot hide your secret from me any longer."

"My secret? What are you talking about?"

"Then tell me that you love me and only me."

"But, I —"

"Sabrina dearest, I know what you yourself cannot even admit. You are in love with Giles."

"No I'm not!" she replied.

"Come. I am no fool, although I will admit that it took his injury to remove the last residue of doubt. You had eyes for no one but him."

"He was unconscious on the floor! I would have rushed Sabrina tried to argue, but could not find the words.

Oliver pulled her hands to his lips and kissed them. "My dear Sabrina, I have trespassed too long on your good graces. If you do not love me as I love you, then I must

leave you to find your heart's desire." He smiled wistfully.
"As it is, this trip to a world of artificial paradise has made
me long for the true paradise of English country life. Some
things can never be replicated."

Sabrina stared at him, relieved and sad at the same
time. She pulled her hands away and pensively studied her
fingers. "But I don't even know how you arrived here,
Oliver, let alone how to send you back."

Chapter 12

Giles came to his senses in a hospital bed, unsure of anything except that he was still alive. Unless this was Hell, which might be the case, because hospitals always inspired him with fear and loathing. He supposed that he probably deserved Hell, given the way he had conducted the last couple of years – before he had moved to Chicago and set his life back on track. He tried to turn his head to gather more information but was tethered to a large number of tubes.

He worked back through his memory trying to assess how he had ended up in this particular Hell. There had been a conference – Farm Con – and a new advertising campaign. Sabrina had been there too. Sabrina. He felt a queer acceleration of his heartbeat and the image of her face, with her luminous blue eyes and soft full lips appeared in his memory.

And Helene. Giles groaned, his memory reactivating all of a sudden. Guy Lord had swung at him. He must have actually connected the punch if Giles was here. Why had Giles ever even talked to Helene? He should have stayed a million miles away.

A nurse came into the room. She had an air of competent efficiency about her. Welcome back, Mr. Philippe. You have had a nice long nap." She adjusted his tubes and then asked him a series of simple questions.

He answered coherently, but his mind still couldn't fully process her words. "Nap?"

"That is a nicer word than medically induced coma," she replied.

"Coma?"

"We needed to make sure your brain wasn't going to swell up. You took quite a hit."

"Yes." He sighed. "So did it?"

"Swell? Yes, it did. So it is a good thing you were out. You seem well oriented in spite of that. But I'll have the neurologist by just the same."

"How long was I out?"

"A little under a week. Now that you are awake, you can tell us if you want us to contact anyone? Friends? Family? I mean, someone might want to come visit."

Giles thought about the question. Who would he want to get a hold of in his time of need? Who would even care? The image of Sabrina came to him again, and he realized with a sudden flash of insight that she was the only person he would want beside him. Somehow, some way, she had become intrinsic to his happiness. This must be love, he realized. He had fallen in love with Sabrina! How had he been so blind? He opened his mouth, ready to tell the nurse to get Sabrina on the phone.

However, Sabrina would have her hands full with the conference. Besides which, he ruefully remembered, she already had a boyfriend very much in love with her. Oliver wouldn't be too thrilled with Sabrina playing nursemaid to a friend. Was that even the right word? He hoped she considered him a friend. But what if she still thought of him only as a work colleague, or, worse yet, a boss? A boss who had crossed the line with her way too many times.

Dear God, he had been a first class idiot. He wished he could take it all back. No, he wouldn't take back that kiss in front of Helene. That kiss had been pure magic. And that incident in the hotel room? He wouldn't take that back either. In fact, he would take it a lot farther if given another chance. Maybe after the conference, he could invite Sabrina out properly and state his case. Oliver be damned.

Good lord. What on earth had happened with Farm Con?

The nurse had clearly been monitoring him. She laid a hand on his arm. "Easy does it. No need to get agitated. I am sure whoever you work with will have taken care of whatever."

"What? You know about Farm Con?"

She nodded. "Everybody in America knows about Farm Con. We have had press camped out in the waiting room since you first got here. That's why we waited until you were awake to ask about visitors. I mean, you will know who is your sister, correct?"

"I don't have a sister."

"Ah. Some reporter has been impersonating your fictitious sister all week."

Giles closed his eyes. This was worse than he could have imagined. Not only was it bad enough that Helene's movie star boyfriend had slugged him in front of a giant room full of people, including the woman he now knew he was in love with, but apparently all of America knew about it as well. He had to get out of this hospital bed as soon as possible and talk to Sabrina. He had to tell her that there was nothing with Helene. And she had to believe him, no matter what the rest of the world told her. Then again, if paparazzi were camped out at the hospital, would they go so far as to camp out at his apartment too?

"I need my phone. I need to get out of here. Please help me," Giles said.

"You will leave here when the doctor says you can leave. Right now, your job is to rest up and heal. No phones."

The rest of the conference felt as if a tornado had picked Sabrina up and carried her aloft, around and around, only to set her back down like Dorothy, dazed and winded. Marilyn arrived to take charge, but her general lack of understanding coupled with a desire to dominate, did not sit well with any of Giles' staff, Marci or the ad agency.

They all threatened mutiny. Things got so tense that several messages went up to the CEO, who finally had to fly to Los Vegas himself and sort it out.

According the office gossip, the CEO pulled Marilyn into a conference room for a meeting. No one was sure what was said at the meeting, but Marilyn subsequently checked out if the hotel and was not heard from since. The next thing Sabrina knew, she received a summons to that very same conference room.

"This is it," she mumbled as she pulled her work-appropriate blazer together and tried to button it. It squeezed her chest like a vice. She sucked in her stomach and opened the door.

The CEO, Red Carson, was a tall man, handsome for someone in his sixties, and oozing that kind of confidence that power seems to give older men. He had ditched the cowboy hat for the interview, but it sat stiffly on a chair beside him. Sabrina felt intimidated immediately.

Red flashed a smile that didn't quite reach his eyes, stood up and extended his hand. "Sabrina March, it is good to finally meet you." He had a faint drawl that seemed appropriate for someone who wore a Stetson hat, but nothing that could be easily identified or ridiculed.

She shook his hand. He had a firm dry grip. So far so good. "Good to meet you as well."

He sat back down and indicated she should do the same in the chair across the table.

She sat down on the edge of the chair, pulling her knees together and keeping her back straight.

Red leaned back in his chair. "I hear that I have you to thank for this new ad campaign idea."

She hesitated, unsure if she should really take the credit. A guy in her place probably would. She nodded, but then added, "Giles and the rest of the group deserve credit too. It was a team effort."

"Yes, I understand. However, Giles may take some time to recover and we need someone on the ground right now that can manage the rest of the conference. I figure you are probably better placed than anyone to do that, so I asking you to step up – way up – and get this across the goal line. Do you think you can handle that?"

Sabrina felt her chest constrict and it wasn't the blazer. Oh lord, could she really manage this? But then a little confident voice, a voice she had silenced one too many times, reasserted itself inside her head. Of course she could handle this. She knew all the ins and outs because she had worked with Giles on everything. He had made sure of it. She felt a rush of gratitude. Giles had brought her to this place, and she couldn't let him down.

"No problem."

"That's just what I want to hear. You do a good job and there is a promotion in it. I like to reward talent, and from what I have seen, Ms. March, you have talent."

Sabrina left the meeting with her head in the clouds. Unfortunately, the feeling of euphoria didn't last long, because the rush of work that came with her new found responsibility threatened to overwhelm her. She dug in and didn't look back.

When the week was finally over, Sabrina and Oliver loaded up their suitcases and set out for the open road. They had had very little time to talk about their situation and Giles' presence hung heavy between them. Sabrina had tried to contact Giles and had even shown up at the hospital, only to be turned away like one of the many reporters still keeping watch in the lobby. She sent texts to his phone, informing him about what she was doing at the conference, but he never answered.

Sabrina felt that the drive home was a bit like a farewell tour – satisfying but bittersweet. Oliver made a good attempt to be his normal inquisitive and cheerful self, but Sabrina could feel the effort it took. They treated each other like roommates and it was only when Sabrina awoke in the morning with his arm around her, that she remembered what he had wanted from her. How was she ever going to send him back to wherever he had come from?

She was looking forward to her own bed and a long hot shower when they finally dragged themselves and their luggage up the stairs to her apartment. She fumbled with the key and then sighed with relief as the door opened. That relief was short-lived, however.

On the floor in front of her, camped out with an odd assortment of bags and a guitar case sat her brother.

"Dave! What are you doing here?"

Dave scrambled up and gave her his best little brother grin. "I hope you don't mind if I crash here for a couple of days. The band is on hiatus. Hey, who is this?" Dave held out his hand to Oliver. "I'm Dave, Sabby's brother."

Sabrina turned to Oliver. "Oliver, this is my younger brother, David. Dave, this is Oliver, my er boyfriend."

Oliver grabbed Dave's hand and shook it warmly. "Delighted to meet a member of my dear Sabrina's family. She has told me so much about you. I too am a lover of music, but fear I have no experience with what do you call your instrument, a guitar? Is it anything like a lute?"

Dave returned the handshake in a friendly way but gave Sabrina a look that clearly said, "Where did you get this guy?"

"Oliver is from England," Sabrina chimed in, as if that explained everything. And then, because there was really no hope if Oliver was allowed to talk, she added, "So the band broke up?"

"It's just a hiatus. Creative differences, solo projects, you know how it is. In any case, I had time so I thought I would come see my favorite sister for a bit. I have my sleeping bag so I can just hang out here." He gestured around the room. "What's for dinner?"

Sabrina sighed. "Nothing at the moment. Why don't you let us unpack and then we can figure out the food situation."

Sabrina took her good sweet time in the shower, afraid of what she would find when she got out. Oliver was sure to have given Dave an earful in her absence. She would brazen it out as long as she could. If worse came to worse, she would have to take Dave aside and explain the situation. He'd known her long enough that he might not immediately question her sanity. In any case, at least he could act as a buffer. The tension with Oliver was wearing.

Dave's credulity lasted somewhat longer than the normal human being. Sabrina supposed that it must be the pot she was pretty sure Dave had smoked when he was with the band, or maybe creatives had a more elastic sense of normal. It wasn't until two weeks had passed that he caught her alone after a long day at work. Oliver had retired early and so they had the rest of the apartment to themselves.

"Don't take this the wrong way, Sabby, but Oliver is a little weird. I mean, he seems like a good guy and he really likes you and all that, but it's like he's lived in a cave or something. He didn't know who the Beatles were or the Stones. And forget the Sex Pistols or Queen. To listen to him, music stopped at Mozart."

"He likes classical music. Is that so wrong?"

"Whatever. I don't care that he doesn't like rock. I'm telling you that he never even heard of the best British rock there is. Didn't know what I was talking about. I had to show him videos on YouTube and even then it didn't register. How can you be from England and not know who the Beatles are? Is he suffering from memory loss or amnesia or something?"

"No." She hesitated and then said, "Look Dave, if I tell you something, will you promise not to call me crazy?"

"When have you ever been crazy? Of the three of us, you have always been the sensible one."

"I know. That's why this is so hard. Oliver is, well, I don't know what or who he is. He just appeared one morning, out of the blue, like the hero from a novel. Actually, the hero from a specific novel called *To Kiss an Earl*. He says he is the Earl of March and I am his wife, Sabrina, because that is his love interest in the book.

Although I don't look anything like the character and am obviously not a Regency woman. I mean, can you see me as Elizabeth Bennet?"

Dave's mouth twisted into a smile. "You have got to be kidding – Oliver was the guy you thought was a friend of mine?"

"Seriously Dave, I don't know what to do. You have to help me."

He let out a whoop of laughter. "Sabby, why does everything have to be so weird with you?"

"I know! But none of it makes any sense. You are sure he is not a friend of yours?"

"Trust me. I don't know any guy that strange. Besides, sounds like kind of a sick joke."

"So what do I do now? I can't just throw him out of my apartment. Where would he go?"

"Tell me from the beginning, exactly what happened."

Sabrina gave him the whole story of Oliver's mysterious appearance, not omitting the fact that she woke up to find him in her bed. She had thought to gloss over that part, but Dave had a way of making her confess the ugly truth.

"Did you sleep with him?" Dave said, clearly curious.

"No, but look at him – I will admit to being tempted. This is so TMI. Can you please get back to helping me figure out how he got here?"

"What about amnesia? He got hit by a bus and wandered in."

"Through my locked door? Besides, who would forget everything but Regency England?"

"Hear me out. He got hit by a bus and wandered into a bar. You picked him up and brought him home but were too drunk to remember it."

"That still doesn't explain the fact that he thinks he is an earl from a book about the 19th century."

"You are both crazy – folie à deux."

"Can you please be serious?" she said.

"I am being serious." He looked at the floor for a while, lost in thought. "This is going to sound completely crazy, but —"

"More crazy than folie à deux?"

"Yes. Maybe they gave you that name for a reason."

"What name?"

"Sabrina."

"I was named for that movie – you know – Audrey Hepburn and Humphrey Bogart. And William Holden plays the younger brother. It was Grandma's favorite film, and after they got Tiffany from *Breakfast at Tiffany's*, I guess mom and dad were all out of ideas."

"That was the party line, but what if it wasn't that Sabrina, but the other one."

"What other one?"

"You know, *Sabrina the Teenage Witch.*"

"What? The TV show?"

Dave stood up and started to pace. "Or the comic book. Just hear me out. Grandma was a little different, right? And you are like the spitting image of her, right?"

"You don't need to point out to me that I didn't end up a tall blonde like Tiffany."

"Okay, so what if the name was a clue to some powers you inherited from Grandma Pearl?"

"So your new theory is that Grandma Pearl was a witch and that after I was born, she realized that I had her powers and so in order to clue me in at a later date, she suggested naming me after a TV character that was also a witch?"

"Yep."

Sabrina started to laugh. "And I have somehow with my magical powers conjured Oliver up out of thin air?"

He nodded.

"So, you are saying that I am a clueless Harry Potter?"

"Basically, yes. There must have been something you did – a series of events that cast a spell and pulled Oliver out of whatever book this is he came from. All you need to do is cast some spell to send him home."

Sabrina was laughing so hard at this point that she could barely breathe. "Okay. Just let me go ahead and do that." She stood up and gave Dave a hug. "Good night. We'll come up with some better ideas in the morning."

Chapter 13

Giles was not a particularly vain man, but he had some idea that his ability to attract women was based on a decently handsome face and a body toned through years of biking. It was somewhat disconcerting therefore to finally catch a glimpse of himself in a mirror when the nurse got him out of bed and took him to the bathroom. His face was thin and drawn. They had shaved his head and there was a nasty line of stitches on one side of his skull. And the billowing dressing gown couldn't hide the fact that he had lost any muscle tone he might have had. Besides that, he was incredibly weak.

He crawled back into the hospital bed feeling defeated. What was he going to do with himself now? Maybe he should go back to Belgium and spend some time licking his wounds and taking stock of his priorities. He could visit his father. It might be good to live the quiet village life for a bit.

The nurse checking his vitals was just about to leave when a knock sounded on the door. "Come in," she said without looking up.

Giles anticipated another nurse or maybe a neurologist, but his jaw dropped open when he saw Red Carson leaning against the door jamb. Shit. This was bad. Giles had never actually been fired, but he supposed the experience wasn't pleasant.

Red was dressed in in a suit, but still wore his white Stetson and black cowboy boots. His expression was inscrutable. "Hope you aren't feeling too sorry for yourself."

"No," Giles replied sheepishly. "I am doing fine. They are telling me I can leave tomorrow."

Red strode up to the bed and eyed the nurse until she got the hint and left. "Good. I swear to God I've never seen such a pack of hyenas as the folks camped out in the waiting room. You have yourself a real media circus."

"How did you get in? They told me no one but family was allowed, and I don't have any family here in the states."

"I had to make some calls. Look Giles, I'll be honest with you. When I hired you to shake things up, I didn't mean this."

Giles felt himself sink lower into the pillows. "I know. Trust me when I say that I never thought I would be clocked by Guy Lord in front of a conference room full of people. I'm sorry to get the company involved like this."

Red studied him a moment and then cracked a smile. "Are you thinking I'm going to fire you?"

"The thought had crossed my mind," Giles replied.

"Well, un-think it. You may not have wanted this attention, but I am not going to let this opportunity go by.

Federal Farm Machinery has gotten more media buzz in the last week than we have ever gotten – good attention too. I have had Marci and Kwame on every morning show and news report. They are great by the way – and just what we need – fresh faces for the brand. I don't know how you found them." He paused. "Besides, how would I look firing a guy who took a punch to the head?"

"I would resign if you needed me to."

"Please don't. You have single-handedly pulled our U.S. marketing out of the dark ages and now I want you to do the same for Europe."

"Europe?"

"Do you have a problem going home? The position is located in Brussels."

"No but, with all due respect —"

"When people say that, it usually means no," Red said.

"It's just that I am so weak right now."

"I get it, and I am more than happy to give you all the time off you need to recover and move. Just tell me you'll take the job."

"Yes, of course."

"Good. Now let's talk about how to break you out of this place. I have the company plane ready to leave whenever you can get yourself discharged."

It took some maneuvering, but Giles finally left the hospital the next day. A car drove him to the plane and he was able to climb up the stairs with some effort. He sank gratefully down in a seat. Red Carson showed up ten minutes later and took seat across from him.

"You look a little better."

Giles reflexively ran his hand over his shaved scalp. He was starting to get a short fuzz. "I'm just glad to be away from the hospital. Look, I don't want to be coddled. Just how bad was Farm Con? I haven't had the heart to even look at my phone. Besides, it has too many texts from numbers I don't recognize."

"Not as bad as you might think given the kickoff. That Marilyn woman showed up and ruffled all sorts of feathers. But once I got in and could size up the situation, I put Sabrina March in charge and she pulled it off." Red leaned in. "You did good work with that one. She has a bright future with Federal Farm Machinery."

Giles felt his chest tighten with pride and affection. Sabrina was the most wonderful woman. "Yes, she does. I don't know what the company has in terms of training, but —"

"We are going to pay for a MBA, and I'm moving her up. She can work with Holly. I've hired her to fill your role on an interim basis until you come back from sorting out our European marketing."

Giles smiled, a great weight lifted off of his shoulders. He hadn't ruined everything. Helene hadn't destroyed his life. He could start over on a better path. He could start over with Sabrina. If Sabrina would have him. If Oliver could be gently moved out of the picture.

He spent a week in his apartment, recuperating and avoiding the press. It was a good thing he lived in a building with decent security and concierge services. He thought about calling Sabrina to see how she was handling everything. He went to do it more than once, but struggled with what to say. He didn't want to make it seem like he was checking up on her – as if he didn't trust her to do a good job. And he certainly wasn't sure how to break it to her that he just might have fallen in love. He needed to get away and think.

Getting away was just a question of taking a flight to Brussels early in the morning. And once in Brussels, he decamped to his father's house in a small town about an hour outside of the capital. His father's girlfriend took one look at him and promptly started cooking a heavy beef stew and Belgian fries. It felt good to be home.

Giles' recovery was slower than he liked, but in time he began to look and feel more like himself. He started his new job and got a flat in Brussels. Despite the fact that Guy Lord was still in the news and facing some potential prison time for assaulting Giles, the businessmen and diplomats who filled the streets of the city took little notice of him. He was able to live just as he chose. It was a blessing that he took full advantage of, getting to know the city again after his stint in the Chicago. Life returned to the rhythm that had been disrupted so disastrously by Helene.

He should have been perfectly content. He should have felt completely whole. He should have been happy. And yet, there was a void in his life that no amount of cosmopolitan living could fill. He thought about Sabrina night and day. He tried, for the sake of his sanity, to engross himself in work and to fill every remaining hour catching up with friends. Unfortunately, no matter what he did, she never left his thoughts. He found it immensely ironic that a woman he had worked beside for so many hours, who he had never seriously thought of, could now occupy him so completely. Besides, Sabrina had given no indication that she wanted to have anything more to do with him. She hadn't contacted him as far as he knew, and certainly hadn't visited the hospital.

And then a thought occurred to him. What if Sabrina had texted him and her text was buried in the thousands of texts he had received and ignored from the press? He searched her name and low and behold, ten texts popped up, unopened. His heart skipped a beat and his finger shook as he opened the first one.

Chapter 14

Dave stayed in Sabrina's apartment for several months. Instead of getting annoyed, Sabrina felt incredibly grateful. His presence buffered the increasing tension between Sabrina and Oliver. Oliver had looked to her for a plan to get home, and she had looked to him for the same, but nothing seemed to work. She started with the many fan sites for Paige Lindsey, but could find no indication that anyone else had ever had one of her characters come to life. In fact, she couldn't find anyone who had ever experienced anything remotely like her situation in the vast expanse of the Internet. And that was very surprising given the weirdness of some of the stuff she found.

She then tried psychics and mediums and other healer-type people who advertised at the back of magazines.

None of them could explain Oliver's appearance or help with his disappearance. Sabrina had even gone so far as to closely examine the floor and wall beside and below her bed to see if there was a trap door of some sort – perhaps a Narnia-like floorboard or a tunnel into another dimension. She even wondered about the real life existence of the Tardis. Perhaps *Dr. Who* wasn't just a television program?

As if Sabrina didn't have enough on her plate! She had come back from Farm Con to a new position and new MBA coursework. She wasn't going to complain about a much better job and more money, particularly when it meant she could stop eating Ramen as a staple food item and could purchase work clothes that gave her figure much needed structure. However, after a long day at work, she felt horrible coming home to Oliver's disappointment.

She poured out her desperation into Becky's willing ears over coffee one Saturday.

"I never thought I would ever hear you talk about getting rid of a boyfriend," Becky said.

"I know, but he seems so miserable. I want to help him, but I am out of ideas."

Becky nodded. "You could send him over to me. I don't mind."

Sabrina smiled. "I know you don't, but it doesn't fix my problem."

Becky took a sip of her caramel latte. "You have walked through everything you did the night before he showed up?"

"Don't tell me you buy into Dave's witch theory," Sabrina replied. "I did not cast a spell."

"Just humor me."

"Okay, okay. I got home after work and found that a package had arrived. It was from my mother and it contained my grandmother's necklace. My mom had found it in the safe deposit."

"This is the grandma you were close to? The one you look like?"

"Yes, Grandma Pearl."

"The necklace is the one you are wearing right now?"

Sabrina nodded. "I wear it all the time."

"Hmm. It looks old. We're you wearing it that night?"

"I know I tried it on when it came, but I would have taken it off before bed."

"Did you?"

"I don't know. Does it matter?"

Becky leaned in conspiratorially. "Did you read *To Kiss an Earl* right before bed?"

"Just what are you getting at?"

"You get a necklace from your grandmother – the one who you resemble and who suggested your name – and

293

that next day a man shows up from a book you are obsessed with. Doesn't it seem like the necklace is connected to Oliver? I mean, he is the man of your dreams."

"He is not the man of my dreams!" Sabrina replied hotly. And then she stopped, suddenly aware of a vague memory from childhood. Grandma Pearl and the necklace. Sabrina had been dreaming of Oliver before he was there when she woke up. And she had forgotten to take the necklace off that night. She remembered now. She had had it on when she escaped to the bathroom to dress for work. "Oh my God, Becky. You may actually be right."

"Of course I am."

And then another thought occurred to Sabrina. How many times had she worn the necklace to bed? She remembered one occasion very clearly – the night in the hotel when Giles opened her door and took her in his arms. She felt her face flush red. She had been having a very steamy dream about him right before – could it be that she had somehow cast a spell on him as well? It certainly explained why Giles would risk his reputation with a nighttime booty call.

"Oh my God," Sabrina said again. "What have I done?"

"What?"

"Becky, I'm not sure I buy this whole witch and spell concept, but it is the only thing that has made any sense. If it is true, then I might have accidentally gotten Giles to come to my hotel room in the middle of the night."

Becky started to laugh. "You mean you were having a dream about him and he showed up?"

Sabrina nodded. "And it was one of those dreams, so —"

Becky's laughter turned into gut-busting guffaws. She wiped her eyes. "Okay, seriously, I want your powers! You have called into being not one but two perfect men."

Sabrina looked at her. "But don't you see how awful this is?"

"Did anything happen with Giles?"

"No, he snapped out of it before we could even kiss. God, what must Giles think of me?"

Becky made a dismissive noise. "And has Oliver been miserable here in this time?"

"Not until it became clear I wasn't in love with him."

"So, no harm no foul. You just need to wear the necklace tonight and dream that Oliver is back home, wherever that is."

"How am I supposed to control my dreams?"

"You've done it twice already."

Sabrina took a large sip of coffee. She couldn't quite believe that she had been brought to this point. Since when had her life become so weird? Since her Regency boyfriend had made his appearance, of course. "I can't believe I am going to say this, but I will give it a try."

Becky patted her hand. "Good girl. Unless you want to send Oliver my way that is."

Sabrina chuckled. "I will give him the option, don't worry."

That night she sat Oliver down on the couch beside her and took his hands in hers. "Oliver dear, I think there might be a way to send you home. I would like to try it tonight, if that is okay with you?"

"What is it?" he replied hopefully.

She touched the necklace at her throat and explained the conversation with Becky.

He looked incredulous. "Surely in this age of science you have a better explanation than this?"

Sabrina shook her head. "I am all out of ideas. At least if this doesn't work, no harm will come to you and me."

"But how can you believe in witchcraft?"

"I don't – at least – not really. I agree that it is a silly thought, but science has given me no way of knowing how you came to be here. The only thing that makes any sense is that I have done it through the power of my desire to live in the world of a book."

"It is a real place, Sabrina."

"I know it is," she said to calm him down. "Look Oliver, I may not get another chance, so I want to tell you everything in my heart. You have given me unconditional love and support and that has meant the world to me."

"Even if you cannot reciprocate my affection?"

She nodded. "We were never meant to be together. Our times are out of sync. This necklace theory may be complete trash, but I have to try. I have to get you back to the world you belong in."

He pulled her hand to his lips and kissed them reverently. "I understand, but I wish it was different."

Sabrina smiled. "So do I Oliver, so do I."

Chapter 15

Giles got to work late and cursed under his breath. It was just like Helene to show up in Brussels, paparazzi in toe. She had appeared unannounced at his apartment and prevented him from leaving for work with dramatic talk of undying devotion. It was more than Giles could stand. How had he ever worshiped at her alter? And then, after finally convincing her to leave, he had been followed by photographers all the way to his office. It was more than a normal person could possibly put up with.

Couldn't she get it through her head that he didn't want to have anything to do with her? Not on the best of days and certainly not when he had a business trip that would conveniently take him to Chicago and into Sabrina's orbit. The trip provided the perfect veneer of work to allow him to gauge Sabrina's receptiveness to a declaration of love. After reading her texts, Giles had finally and irrevocably decided to be true to himself and take his chances.

Giles stowed his bag under his desk and dug into his work, determined to put all thoughts of Helene out of his mind. The flight to Chicago left in a couple of hours. He stared at the computer with laser-like focus and succeeded so well that he jumped when his administrative assistant knocked on his door.

She stuck her head in his office. "The car is here for the airport. And I think you should know that photos of you and Helene St. Just are all over the Internet gossip sites again. Take care at the airport."

Giles groaned, but he picked up his bag anyway, resigned to his fate. It was worth anything to finally know if he had any future with Sabrina. Fortunately, he didn't have any media following him to his gate. However, when he arrived, he realized that they had been following another airline passenger, namely Helene.

He hurried onto the plane. "What are you doing here?" he said suspiciously as she boarded and sat down beside him in first class.

Helene adjusted a pair of large dark sunglasses on her nose. "I have a meeting in Chicago and this was the only seat left. Besides, if you wanted privacy, you should have flown in a private jet."

He shook his head. "Fine, but I warn you, I am going to put my headphones on and ignore you the whole trip."

She pulled off the glasses and gave him a look that in the past would have made his blood boil with lust. "Giles." She laid a hand on his arm. "You know that I had nothing to do with Guy hitting you. I would have stopped him if I had known. You have to believe me."

"I do. Helene, you are not to blame for your Cro-Magnon boyfriend. However, as I have told you a million times, I don't want to get back together with you. I have a new life now. I can't return to where we were."

She smiled seductively. "Yes you can. We had some amazing times together."

Giles smiled in response. "Yes, but I'm over that now." He popped his headphones on and closed his eyes.

Giles woke with a start as the plane began the landing sequence. He looked around. Helene stared at her phone, angrily ignoring him. So much the better. Giles dug his phone out of his computer bag and pulled up his email. He had a car waiting for him and a suite in one of the fancy hotels reserved for the week. The sooner he got away from Helene, the better.

Escaping Helene was easier said than done. She refused to exit the plane until everyone else had gotten off and, as he couldn't climb over her, he had to wait too. That meant that they walked off the plane together and into a crowd of people, taking cell phone photos. This was followed by members of the press, who tailed them through the airport and into baggage claim. Giles ignored the flashes of photos and retrieved his suitcase with grim determination. He found his driver as soon as possible and hurried the man out of the terminal.

Sabrina sat in her new office and scanned the proofs for the enhanced web campaign. Today was the day that she would finally see Giles again. Her mind was in a million places but mostly in that fancy New York restaurant, kissing Giles with reckless abandon. She had to get a hold on her emotions. Given everything she had seen on the Internet, she was pretty sure he had patched things up with Helene. She sat back in her chair and looked around, willing her mind to suppress those New York memories. She still couldn't really believe that her life had done such a complete turn in such a short time. She looked down and brushed a piece of lint off of her skirt. It was part of a proper suit. She had several proper suits now.

She looked out the window. The sky appeared leaden, as if rain couldn't be far away. That was how she had been feeling lately, she realized, as if something was about to break. She supposed it was losing Oliver. She touched her grandmother's necklace, still unwilling to believe that it had the power to call forth her Regency boyfriend. And yet, the very night she had decided to try and send Oliver home, she had had a dream. She and Oliver stood in a meadow, the sun shining down on them and a soft breeze blowing the hair around her face. In the distance she could see a vast manor house.

Oliver took her hands in his. "My Sabrina, you have brought me home." He turned her palms up, placing a reverent kiss in the middle of each one.

"I will never forget you," Sabrina replied.

"Nor I you," he said. They stood there for some minutes, gazing at each other. Sabrina had half a mind to ask him if she could stay in this Regency world, but knew in her heart of hearts that she could not give up her old life for some romantic dream. She remained silent, the spell of *To Kiss an Earl* irretrievably broken.

"I must leave," Oliver said. He bowed low over her hands.

Sabrina disengaged her fingers and responded with a deep curtsey. "God speed, dearest Oliver."

"God speed, my lovely Sabrina," he replied.

Oliver turned and walked slowly away from her towards the house. She watched him until she could no longer see his tall form and then woke up, startled and disoriented. She was alone in her bed.

Sabrina tried not to miss him, but it proved impossible. He had been so much a part of her life that she felt his absence keenly. She realized that while she hadn't been in love with him, she had liked him very much and his friendship was impossible to replace.

Fortunately, she had long hours at work and even longer hours with her classes at night. She filled her days with so much activity that her regret at sending Oliver home only lasted the couple of minutes between when her head hit the pillow and she fell soundly asleep. And when asleep, her dreams were mostly of another man, equally elusive and out of reach.

"Hey, no time to daydream. We've got the folks from Europe here in a bit," Holly said.

Sabrina spun around. "I know. I was just thinking about the meeting and trying to get my head on straight."

Holly stood in the doorway, her arms crossed. "Thinking about Giles?"

Sabrina forced a neutral smile. "Of course. I hope he is fully recovered. It will be great to work with him again."

"I think he is recovered." Holly fiddled with her phone and then held it up. "TMZ is reporting that he arrived in Chicago with Helene St. Just."

"Really?" Sabrina felt her stomach turn over, but pulled herself together. Of course Giles was with Helene. Isn't that what he always wanted? She knew that better than anyone.

Holly walked over to Sabrina's desk and showed her the photos of them walking side by side through the airport.

"Hmm," Sabrina said. "He looks thinner and his hair is short."

"Well, I hope he's happy. If he had to get punched in the head, at least he got the girl."

Sabrina nodded. "I'm sure he is." But she sounded unconvinced even to her own ears.

The meeting was scheduled in the conference room usually reserved for board meetings, with a large picture window overlooking the city. Sabrina got there early and took a seat facing the door. She steeled herself. It was just Giles. She needed to keep her emotions under tight control.

She heard his voice before she saw him and was not prepared for the visceral reaction his soft silky accent had on her. Her cheeks flushed and blood seemed to rush through her veins. Giles could make anything sound like a caress. She poured herself a glass of water and drank it down.

And then he was in the room. They made eye contact and he smiled at her. Her legs turned to mush, and so she pushed herself out of the chair with her hands. Giles made his way to her, greeting this person and that person.

Finally, he took her outstretched hand in his.

"Sabrina," he said. "It is so very good to see you

again."

She mumbled something incoherent and returned

his strong handshake.

He moved on to the next person. Sabrina sat

down, strangely deflated. This was going to be a long

meeting.

Giles spent the entire meeting surreptitiously

studying Sabrina. He had been immediately struck with her

radiant beauty. It was as if he had never really looked at her

before. She'd pulled her dark hair up, exposing the smooth

whiteness of her long neck. She wasn't wearing glasses and

when her exquisite blue eyes focused on him for a moment,

he felt he could get lost in their depths. Sabrina had chosen

to wear red lipstick, and Giles couldn't help but focus

obsessively on the curve of her full lips. Sabrina wore a

fitted suit that hugged her body and a shirt that opened at her throat. It wasn't that the outfit was inappropriate for work, but the merest hint of the breasts beneath the shirt forced him to turn away and focus.

When the meeting broke up, he tried to maneuver around to speak to her but she eluded him and escaped back to her office. Red Carson dragged Giles to a meeting, and when Giles escaped from that, Sabrina's office door was shut. The door remained closed the rest of the day. He came back at five o'clock, but she had already left. Giles decamped to the hotel to lick his wounds. Sabrina clearly did not want to see him.

Chapter 16

It was at least nine o'clock when Sabrina wearily opened the front door to her apartment. She set her bag down on the floor and kicked off her shoes. She hadn't had a chance to eat before class and had an hour of homework yet to do. She pulled a frozen dinner out of the freezer and stuck it in the microwave. Then she wandered back to her bedroom to change into sweatpants. As she had little incentive to pick up with Oliver gone, her clothes were thrown about. She found a tee shirt on the floor and put it on. Then she dug the sweatpants out of a basket of clean clothes.

She walked back to the kitchen and pulled her dinner out of the microwave. She opened her computer on the counter and stood eating, slowing reviewing her MBA homework. She tried not to think about Giles. Despite the short hair and the thin face, he was just as handsome as he had ever been. More so now that she had finally admitted to herself how much she wanted him. She just had to pull herself together. Nothing was ever going to happen with him, and she needed to be able to work with him as a colleague going forward – or at least for the week he was in Chicago.

The intercom buzzed, jolting her out of her fruitless reverie. "Hello?"

"Sabrina?"

Sabrina's heart sped up so fast, that she thought it might burst out of her chest. "Giles? What are you doing here?"

"Can I come up?"

"Yes, of course," she replied, totally flustered. "Sure." She hit the button.

Oh my God! She looked around her apartment and frantically grabbed at a sweater thrown over the couch and retrieved a dirty dish on the coffee table. Then she caught a look at herself in a mirror. Her hair was pulled up in a messy bun, she had eaten off most of her lipstick, and her eyeshadow had smudged. She threw the dish in the sink and the sweater into her room, but she heard the knock at the door before she could address the make-up situation. Whatever. She had to calm down.

She took a couple of deep breaths and walked slowly to the door. She did another round of deep breaths as she unlatched the chain. And then she was face to face with Giles.

He seemed taller somehow standing in her doorway, and she remembered that she was barefoot. He was dressed casually, but neatly, with clothes that hung a little loose on his slimmer frame. He had a few more wrinkles around the eyes, but otherwise seemed well enough.

He smiled nervously. "I am sorry to come here, but I just had to speak with you. I missed you at the office."

Sabrina touched her necklace self-consciously. She hadn't been asleep. God help her if she was now casting spells while awake. "Okay, come in, come in. No problem." She watched him warily and closed the door behind him.

"This is a nice apartment," he said.

"It's okay. An elevator would be nice."

Giles nodded and looked down at the ground.

"How are you feeling? You look good," Sabrina said. That had not come out the way she had intended. She flushed bright red. "I mean, you look like you are recovering."

He looked up and searched her face. There was a pregnant pause. "How is Oliver?"

315

"He went home," she replied.

"So you are doing the long-distance thing now?"

Sabrina sighed. "No, we realized that we weren't right for each other. He was homesick too."

"Oh." Giles looked deep into her eyes. "Sabrina, I would really appreciate it if, whatever I say to you in the next two minutes, you would not rat me out to Human Resources."

Sabrina laughed. "What can you possibly have to say that would make me run to HR now?"

He smiled. "Only that I am wholly and completely and irrevocably in love with you."

Sabrina couldn't quite comprehend. "What?" She pinched her own arm to make sure this wasn't a magical dream.

Giles reached out and grabbed her hand. "That was a bad start. I am in love with you. I've been in love with you for a long time, but couldn't bring myself to tell you until I felt strong enough to brave your rejection."

"But aren't you in love with Helene? TMZ says so."

He pulled her close to him and put his other hand on her shoulder. "So you are going to believe TMZ over me?"

His eyes bored into hers. Sabrina's pulse raced so fast that she felt lightheaded.

"I know you are probably still upset from your break-up with Oliver, but tell me, do I have a chance? Could you ever feel something for me?"

"You are sure I am not asleep?"

"No, of course not. Come on Sabrina, I am in agony."

She returned his gaze, giving him a small taste of the desire she had felt for him almost from the very moment they met. He pulled her into a tight embrace. Their lips met. His mouth was warm and insistent and Sabrina

felt as if the world fell away. She deepened the kiss.

After a minute, Giles pulled back. He cupped her

face in his hands. "Sabrina, my God, I have never wanted

anyone the way I want you. You have no idea what a spell

you have cast on me."

Sabrina smiled up into his handsome face, sure that

she could never feel as happy as she felt in that moment.

"Oh, I think I might."

ACKNOWLEDGMENTS

I would like to thank my family, especially my mother, for giving me editorial assistance and keeping me going even when I don't feel like putting pen to paper. Thanks to my awesome fans in Marshfield, St. Louis and around the country. I really appreciate your support. And finally, I want to thank my colleagues and friends at Security Health Plan and the Marshfield Clinic Health System for their support of my writing career.

ABOUT THE AUTHOR

Lisa Boero is a practicing corporate lawyer who moonlights as a novelist. Her first three books, **Murderers and Nerdy Girls Work Late** and **Bombers, Nerdy Girls Do Brunch** and **Kidnappers and Nerdy Girls Tie the Knot**, feature the fast-talking, face-blind detective Liz Howe. **Hell Made Easy**, blends her legal knowledge, matchless dark humor, and one of her all-time favorite story lines – lawyers trying to outwit the devil. And the first two books of the Lady Althea Mystery Series, **The Richmond Thief** and **The Ranleigh Question**, follow the exploits of Regency England's premier lady scientist as she uses her powers of deduction to unravel even the most complicated mysteries.

Boero lives with her family in Marshfield, Wisconsin, and can be found online at www.lisaboero.com and on her Facebook page, www.facebook.com/authorlisaboero or you can follow Liz Howe on Twitter @Liz_NerdyGirl.